In Good Company

In Good Company

CEDRIC YAMANAKA

A LATITUDE 20 BOOK
UNIVERSITY OF HAWAI'I PRESS
HONOLULU

Printed in the United States of America

07 06 05 04 03   6 5 4 3 2

Library of Congress Cataloging-in-Publication Data
Yamanaka, Cedric.
  In good company / Cedric Yamanaka.
    p. cm.
  "A Latitude 20 Book."
  ISBN 0–8248–2498–9 (pbk. : alk. paper)
  1. Hawaii—Social life and customs—Fiction.   I. Title.

PS3625.A67   I5   2002
813'.6—dc21   2001046287

Some of these stories first appeared elsewhere in slightly different forms:
"What the Ironwood Whispered," in *Hawaii Review* (1985); "One Evening in
the Blue Light Bar and Grill," in HONOLULU magazine (1992); "The Lemon
Tree Billiards House," in *Into the Fire: Asian American Prose*, an anthology
published by The Greenfield Review Press (1996); "The Day Mr. Kaahunui
Rebuilt My Old Man's Fence," in *Mānoa* (1998); "Da Papah Fooball
Champion," in *Bamboo Ridge* (2001).

University of Hawai'i Press books are printed on acid-free
paper and meet the guidelines for permanence and
durability of the Council on Library Resources.

Designed by Trina Stahl

Printed by Versa Press, Inc.

For Ma, Laurie, Caleb, and Grandma Wini

———————

Contents

Acknowledgments

With *mahalo* to:

Pops.

Boston University, especially Leslie Epstein. Without you, none of this would've happened.

The University of Hawai'i at Mānoa, particularly Ian Mac-Millan and Craig Howes for guiding and encouraging a young writer from Kalihi.

The University of Hawai'i Press and my editor Masako Ikeda, for your hard work.

My fine teachers at Kapālama Elementary School, Kalākaua Intermediate School, and Farrington High School.

The Ishimoto family, for always being there.

My new family, especially Wayne, Dwight, and Kathy.

Casey, Nathan, and Tom, for your time in reading the manuscript —and for your friendship over the years.

Time spent with you all is the definition of being in good company.

The Lemon Tree Billiards House

THE LEMON TREE Billiards House is on the first floor of an old concrete building on King Street, between Aloha Electronics and Uncle Phil's Flowers. The building is old and the pool hall isn't very large—just nine tables, a ceiling fan, and a soda machine. No one seems to know how the place got its name. Some say it used to be a Korean bar. Others say it was a funeral home. But all seem to agree that it has a lousy name for a pool hall. At one point someone circulated a petition requesting the name be changed. But Mr. Kong, the proud owner, wouldn't budge. He said his pool hall would always be called the Lemon Tree Billiards House.

Mr. Kong keeps his rates very reasonable. For two dollars an hour, you can hit all of the balls you want. One day I was in there playing eight ball with a sixty-eight-year-old parking attendant. The guy played pretty well—I was squeezing for a while—but he missed a tough slice and left me enough openings to clear the table and sink the eight ball. I won twenty bucks.

Another guy walked up to me. He had a mustache, a baseball cap, and a flannel shirt.

"My name Hamilton," he said. "I ain't too good—but what—you like play?"

I ain't too good. *Sure.*

"My name's Mitch," I said. "Let's play."

We agreed on fifty bucks. Hamilton racked the balls. I broke. It was a good one. The sound of the balls cracking against each other was like a hundred glass jars exploding.

As three striped balls—the nine, twelve, and fifteen—shot into three different pockets, I noticed a good-looking girl in a black dress sitting on a stool in the corner. I don't know if I was imagining it or not but I thought I caught her looking my way. I missed an easy shot on the side pocket. I'd burned my finger cooking saimin and couldn't get a good grip on the cue stick.

"Oh, too bad," said Hamilton. "Hard luck! I thought you had me there." He was what I call a talker. The kind of guy who can't keep his mouth shut. The kind of guy who treats a game of pool like a radio call-in show.

Anyway, Hamilton hit four balls in but stalled on the fifth. I eventually won the game.

Afterward, the girl in the black dress walked up to me.

"Hi," she said, smiling.

"Hello," I said.

"You're pretty good," she said.

"Thanks."

"You wanna play my dad?"

"Who's your dad?"

"You wanna play or not?"

"Who is he?"

"He'll give you five hundred bucks if you beat him."

"Let's go."

I'M A POOL hustler and the Lemon Tree Billiards House is my turf. You see, I've been playing pool all my life. It's the only thing I know how to do. My dad taught me the game before they threw him in jail. I dropped out of school, left home, and traveled around the country challenging other pool players. I've played the best. Now I'm home.

All right, all right. I'm not a pool hustler. I'm a freshman at the University of Hawai'i. And my dad's not in jail. He's an accountant. And I never challenged players around the country. I did play a game in Waipahu once.

I have been playing pool for a while, though. Sometimes I do real well. Sometimes I don't. That's how the game is for me. Four things can happen when I pick up a cue stick. One, sometimes I feel like I'll win and I win. Two, sometimes I feel like I'll win and I lose. Three, sometimes I feel like I'll lose and I lose. Four, sometimes I feel like I'll lose and I win.

I'll tell you one thing, though. I could've been a better pool player if I hadn't been cursed. Yes, cursed.

It all happened back when I was seven years old. My dad had taken me to a beach house. I'm not sure where it was. Somewhere near Mālaekahana, maybe. I remember walking along the beach and seeing some large boulders. I began climbing on the rocks, trying to get a good look at the ocean and the crashing waves. The view was stunning. The water was so blue. And I thought I spotted some whales playing in the surf offshore.

All of a sudden, my father came running down the beach. "Mitch!" he said. "Get off da rocks! Da rocks sacred! No climb up there! No good!"

Ever since that day, I've lived with a curse. One day in the eighth grade, I dropped a touchdown pass and we lost a big intramural football game. I smashed my first car three minutes after I drove it off the lot. My first girlfriend left me for a guy in prison she read about in the papers. I'm the kind of guy who will throw down four queens in a poker game, only to watch helplessly as some clown tosses down four kings. If I buy something at the market, it'll go on sale the next day.

It hasn't been easy. The only thing I do okay is play eight ball. But I could've been better. If it just weren't for this curse.

———————

I DON'T KNOW why I agreed to play pool with this strange girl's father. Maybe it was because she was so beautiful. The best-looking woman I've ever seen. Six feet, two hundred pounds, hairy legs, mustache. Okay, okay. So she wasn't *that* beautiful. Let's just say she was kind of average.

Anyway, we got into her car and she drove toward the Wai'anae coast. She had one of those big black sedans you saw in the seventies. The kind Jack Lord used to drive to 'Iolani Palace in *Hawai'i Five-0*. In about a half hour or so, we wound up at a large beach house with water mills and bronze Buddhas in the yard. Everywhere you looked, you saw trees. Mango, avocado, papaya, banana.

"My dad likes to plant things," the girl explained.

We walked past a rock garden and a koi pond, and she led me into a room with a pool table. There were dozens of cues lined up neatly on the wall, just like at the Lemon Tree Billiards House.

"You can grab a stick," the girl said. "I'll go get my dad."

In a few minutes I realized why she didn't want to tell me who her father was. I was standing face-to-face with Locust Cordero. *The* Locust Cordero. All six-five, 265 pounds of him. Wearing, of all things, a purple tuxedo with a red carnation in the lapel. Locust Cordero, who stood trial for the murder-for-hire deaths of three Salt Lake gamblers several years back. I was about to play eight ball with a hit man.

"Howzit," he said. "*Mahalo*s for coming. My name Locust."

What should I say? I know who you are? I've heard of you? I've seen your mug shots on TV? Congratulations on your recent acquittal? Nice tuxedo?

"Nice to meet you, sir," I said, settling on the conservative. "I'm Mitch."

We shook hands. He wore a huge jade ring on his finger.

"My daughter says you pretty good."

"I try, sir."

"How you like my tuxedo?" he said.

"Nice," I said.

"Shaka, ah?" he said, running his hands over the material. "Silk, brah. Just bought 'em. What size you?"

"What?"

"What size you?" he repeated, opening up a closet. I was stunned. There must have been two dozen tuxedos in there. All sizes. All colors. Black, white, maroon, pink, blue, red. "Here," said Locust, handing me a gold one. "Try put dis beauty on."

"Uh," I said. "How about the black one?"

Again, I was leaning toward the conservative.

"Whatevahs," said Locust, shrugging.

I changed in the bathroom. It took me awhile because I'd never worn a tuxedo before. When I walked out, Locust smiled.

"Sharp," he said. "Look at us. Now we *really* look like pool players."

Locust chalked his cue stick. He was so big, the stick looked like a toothpick in his hands.

"Break 'em, Mitch."

"Yes, sir."

I walked to the table and broke. I did it real fast. I don't like to think about my shots too long. That always messes me up. *Crack!* Not bad. Two solid balls shot into the right corner pocket.

"Das too bad," said Locust, shaking his head.

"Why's that, sir?" I asked.

"Cause," said Locust, "I hate to lose."

———

ONE DAY NOT too long before, I'd visited an exorcist. To get rid of my curse. He was an old Hawaiian man in his late forties or early fifties, recommended to me by a friend. When I called for an appointment, he said he couldn't fit me in. There were a lot of folks out there with problems, I guessed. I told him it was an emergency.

"Okay, come ovah," he said. "But hurry up."

I drove to his house. He lived in Pālolo Valley. I was very scared. What would happen? I could see it now. As soon as I walked into the room, the man would scream and run away from me. He'd tell me he saw death and destruction written all over my face. The wind would blow papers all over his room, and I'd be speaking weird languages I had never heard before and blood and mucus would pour out my mouth.

But nothing like that happened. I walked into his house, expecting to see him chanting or praying. Instead he was sitting behind a koa desk in a Munsingwear shirt and green polyester pants.

"Dis bettah be good," he said. "I went cancel my tee time at Ala Wai for you."

I smiled. I told him my plight. I started from the beginning—telling him about the day I climbed on the rocks and the bad luck I've had ever since.

"You ain't cursed," the man said. He bent down to pick something up from the floor. What was it? An ancient amulet? A charm? None of the above. It was a golf club. An eight iron. "Da mind is one very powerful ting," he said, waving the eight iron around like a magician waving a wand. "It can make simple tings difficult and difficult tings simple."

"What about the rocks?" I said.

"Tink positive," the man said. "You one negative buggah. Da only curse is in your mind."

That's it? No reading scripture? No chanting?

"I tell you one ting, brah," the Hawaiian man said. "One day, you going encountah one challenge. If you beat 'em, da curse going be *pau*. But if you lose, da rest of your life going shrivel up like one slug aftah you pour salt on top."

"Anything else?" I said.

"Yeah," said the Hawaiian man. "You owe me twenty bucks."

———

LOCUST AND I had played ten games. We'd agreed on eleven. I'd won five, he'd won five. In between, his daughter brought us fruit punch and smoked marlin. It was already dark, and I had an oceanography test the next day.

In the final game, I hit an incredible shot—the cue ball jumping over Locust's ball, like a fullback leaping over a tackler, and hitting the seven into the side pocket. This seemed to piss Locust off. He came right back with a beauty of his own—a massé I couldn't believe. In a massé, the cue ball does bizarre things on the table after being hit—like weaving between balls as if it has a mind of its own. Those are the trick shots you see on TV. Anyway, Locust hit a massé, where the cue ball hit not one, not two, not three, but four of his balls into four different holes. *Come on!* I was convinced Locust could make the cue ball spell his name across the green velvet sky of the pool table.

Pretty soon it was just me, Locust, and the eight ball. I looked at Locust real fast, and he stared at me like a starving man sizing up a Diner's chicken *katsu* plate lunch. I took a shot, but my arm felt like a lead pipe and I missed everything. Locust took a deep breath, blew his shot, and swore in three different languages. It was my turn.

And then I realized it. This was the moment that would make or break me. The challenge the exorcist guy was talking about. I had to win.

I measured the table, paused, and said the words that would change my life and save me from shriveling up like a slug with salt poured on it.

"Eight ball. Corner pocket."

I would have to be careful. Gentle. It was a tough slice to the right corner pocket. If I hit the cue ball too hard, it could fall into the wrong pocket. That would be a scratch. I would lose.

I took a deep breath, cocked my stick, and aimed. I hit the cue ball softly. From here, everything seemed to move in slow motion. The cue ball tapped the eight ball and the eight ball seemed to take hours to roll toward the hole. Out of the corner of my eye, I saw Locust's daughter standing up from her seat, her hands covering her mouth.

CLACK. *Plop.*

The ball fell into the hole. The curse was lifted. I had won. I would have been a happy man if I hadn't been so damned scared.

Locust walked up to me, shaking his head. He reached into his pocket. Oh, no. Here it comes. He was gonna take out his gun, shoot me, and bury my body at some deserted beach. Good-bye, cruel world. Thanks for the memories . . .

"I no can remembah da last time I lost," he said, pulling out his wallet and handing me five crispy one-hundred-dollar bills. "*Mahalos* for da game."

———

LOCUST ASKED ME to stay and talk for a while. We sat on straw chairs next to the pool table. The place was dark except for several gaslit torches hissing like leaky tires. Hanging on the walls were fishing nets and dried, preserved fish, lobsters, and turtles.

"You must be wondering why we wearing dese tuxedos," said Locust.

"Yeah," I said.

"Well, dis whole night, it's kinda one big deal for me." Locust leaned toward me. "You see, brah, I nevah leave my house in five years."

"Why?" I said. I couldn't believe it.

"All my life, everybody been scared of me," said Locust, sighing. "Everywheah I go, people look at me funny. Dey whispah behind my back."

"But—"

"Lemme tell you someting," he continued. "Dey went try me for murder coupla times. Both times, da jury said I was innocent. Still, people no like Locust around. Dey no like see me. And das why I nevah step foot outta dis place."

"Forgive me for saying so, sir," I said. "But that's kinda sad. That's no way to live."

"Oh, it ain't dat bad," said Locust. "I play pool. I go in da ocean, spear *uhu*. I throw net for mullet. Once in a while, I go in da mountains behind da house and shoot me one pig . . ."

"But don't you ever miss getting out and walking around the city? Experiencing life?"

I was getting nervous again. I mean, here I was, giving advice on how to live to Locust Cordero. After I had just beaten the guy at eight ball.

"Whasso great about walking around da streets of da city?" said Locust after a while. "People shooting and stabbing each othah. Talking stink about each othah. Stealing each othah's husbands and wives. Breaking each othah's hearts."

"You scared?" I said, pressing my luck.

"Yeah," said Locust, looking me straight in the eye, "I guess I am."

We didn't say anything for a while. I could hear the waves of the ocean breaking on the beach.

"So," said Locust, shifting in his seat, "where you went learn to shoot pool?"

"The Lemon Tree Billiards House," I said.

"Da Lemon Tree Billiards House?" Locust said, shaking his head. "What kine name dat? Sound like one funeral home."

"Sir," I said, "I'm sorry. Can I say something?"

"Sure."

"You're living your life like a prisoner. You might as well have been convicted of murder and locked in jail."

Yeah, sometimes it seems I just don't know when to shut up.

"Evah since I was one kid, I had hard luck," said Locust, moving closer to me and whispering. "You see, I'm cursed."

"You're what?" I said, surprised.

"I'm cursed," Locust repeated, raising his voice. "Jeez, for one young kid, you get lousy hearing, ah? Must be all dat loud music you buggahs listen to nowadays."

"How'd you get cursed?" I said.

"One day, when I was one kid, I was climbing some rocks looking out at da ocean. Down Mālaekahana side. All of a sudden, my bruddah start screaming, 'Get down from there. No good. Da rocks sacred.' "

I couldn't believe it. Locust and I were cursed by the same rocks. We were curse brothers.

"Da ting's beat me," said Locust, shaking his head.

"You're talking like a loser."

"A what?" said Locust, getting out of his chair.

"Locust," I said, my voice cracking, "I lived with the same curse and I beat it."

"How?" said Locust, sitting back down. "I tried everyting. Hawaiian salt. Ti leaves. Da works."

"You gotta believe in yourself."

"How you do dat?"

"With your mind," I said. "See, the first thing you gotta do is meet a challenge and beat it," I said. "Go outside. Walk the streets. Meet people."

"You evah stop for tink how dangerous da world is?" said Locust. "Tink about it. How many tings out there are ready, waiting, for screw you up. Death, sickness, corruption, greed, old age . . ."

It was scary. Locust was starting to make sense.

"I don't know," I finally said.

"Tink about it," said Locust. "Tink about it."

ONE DAY SEVERAL weeks later, I was playing eight ball at the Lemon Tree Billiards House. Several people were arguing about the source of an unusual smell. Some said it came from a cardboard box filled with rotten *choy sum* outside on the sidewalk in front of the pool hall. Others said it was Kona winds blowing in the pungent smell of *taegu* from Yuni's Bar-B-Q. Still others said the peculiar smell came from Old Man Rivera, who sat in a corner eating a lunch he had made at home. Too much *patis*—fish sauce—in his *sari sari*.

"If you like good smell," said Mr. Kong, the owner of the Lemon Tree Billiards House, "go orchid farm. If you like play pool, come da Lemon Tree Billiards House."

I was on table number three with a young Japanese guy with short hair. He had dark glasses and wore a black suit. He looked like he was in the *yakuza*.

I had already beaten three guys. I was on a roll. It gets like that every now and then. When you know you can't miss.

The *yakuza* guy never smiled. And everytime he missed a shot, he swore at himself. Pretty soon he started to hit the balls very hard —thrusting his cue stick like a samurai spearing an opponent. He was off, though, and I eventually won the game.

"You saw how I beat the *yakuza* guy?" I said to Mr. Kong, who was now on a stepladder unscrewing a burned-out lightbulb.

"*Yakuza* guy?" said Mr. Kong. "What *yakuza* guy?"

"The Japanese guy in the suit," I said.

"Oh," said Mr. Kong, laughing like crazy. "You talking about

Yatsu! Das my neighbor. He ain't no *yakuza.* He one preschool teachah!"

Just then, Locust Cordero walked into the Lemon Tree Billiards House. Mr. Kong stopped laughing. Everyone stopped their games. No one said a word. The only sound I heard was the ticking of a clock on the wall.

"Mitch," said Locust, "I went take your advice. I no like live like one prisonah no more."

I was speechless.

"You know what dey say," said Locust. "Feel like one five-hundred-pound bait has been lifted from my shoulders."

"Weight," I said.

"For what?" said Locust, obviously confused.

"No, no," I said. "Five hundred pound *weight.* Not bait."

"Whatevahs," said Locust. "Da curse is gone."

He walked over to one of Mr. Kong's finest tables, ran his thick fingers over the smooth wood, and looked into the deep pockets like a child staring down a mysterious well.

"Eight ball?" he asked, turning to me.

"Yeah," I said, smiling. "Yeah, sure."

One Evening in the Blue Light Bar and Grill

ALL CLARENCE KALILIKANE, the Coffinmaker, wanted when he walked into the Blue Light Bar and Grill on Hotel Street was a cold beer. The smell of *kalbi,* sashimi, and Pine-Sol lingered in the air. A stuffed marlin hung on the wall above a shelf lined with wine bottles. Several people sat at the bar, slouched over their glasses, watching the wrestling matches on television. It was a tag-team match. Two guys in masks—the Brothers of Doom—were taking on a guy with long hair and a guy with a chain around his neck. Clarence thought about leaving, but it was too late.

The waitress brought Clarence his beer, and he gave her two crisp dollar bills.

"Eh," she said, "I know you."

"No," said Clarence, "I tink you mistaken."

"You somebody, ah?"

"No, I . . ."

"Aaaaaugh!" she said. "Aaaaugh! Oh, my goodness! Everybody look! Da Coffinmaker is here!"

That's all it took. Everyone turned around. A silence fell over the Blue Light Bar and Grill.

A man in a colorful aloha shirt took out a magazine from

his back pocket. It was the spring issue of *Wrestling World,* with Clarence on the cover. Blaisdell Arena. His forehead was being banged against the turnbuckle of the ring by Nikolai the Terrible. Nikolai the Terrible ate aluminum cans and sang the Russian national anthem before each match. Clarence winced when he saw the magazine cover. It was a bad picture.

"Could you sign dis?" the man said. It almost looked like he was bowing. "For my son?"

"Sure. What's your son's name?"

"Charley. Charley Souza."

"Charley Souza?" said the waitress. "Same name as you?"

"Put 'To my best friend, Charley Souza.' "

Clarence was, by now, the man of the hour. Everyone came to talk wrestling with him. Clarence struggled through discussions about his cage match with Kuhio the Bloodsucker, the time Wally the Ripper opened up Clarence's head with brass knuckles, his Indian Death Match with the Mad Apache. It was incredible. Everyone in the Blue Light Bar and Grill seemed to have followed Clarence's exploits. The tag-team match on television was in the second fall now. The men in the masks—the Brothers of Doom—were winning. One of them had the guy with long hair in a figure four leg-lock.

"Coffinmaker," said Charley, "I watch you all da time on television. I tink you was robbed in dat grudge match with Da Beast with Four Fingers."

"Please, call me Clarence."

"I tell you, Coffinmaker, er, Clarence, sir, you had dat bastard on da ropes. How could dey let Butcher Hookano interfere in da match and whack you on da head with one folding chair? I mean, how could dey?"

"I . . ."

"There ain't no justice in da world. There ain't no justice."

Clarence sipped at his beer.

"Eh!" someone said. "Look at da TV!"

Clarence Kalilikane looked at the television and almost died. The tag-team match was over. The Brothers of Doom had won. They were now broadcasting the main event. It was a match Clarence had several months ago with the Incredible Dagoo. The Incredible Dagoo was a man with thirty-five-inch biceps who had shaped his incisors with a nail file into fangs. While the Incredible Dagoo bit and chewed at the ropes of the ring, Clarence blew kisses to the crowd.

"Just tink," someone at the bar said, "da Coffinmaker here. In da Blue Light Bar and Grill."

"Sorry to do dis, folks," said the bartender, "but it's nine o'clock."

"Can't she wait?" someone screamed.

"Afraid not," said the bartender. He turned the television off. "Nine o'clock is nine o'clock."

The lights dimmed and a recorded voice announced, "Ladies and gentlemen, for your listening pleasure, da Blue Light Bar and Grill is proud to present Miss Leimomi Sanchez."

A tall woman, almost six feet, in a long dress with gold glitter walked onto a tiny stage next to the bar. There was a patter of polite applause. She picked up a microphone and, accompanied by a guy in a tuxedo playing the piano, began to sing: *"Moon River, wider than a mile . . ."* She had a very deep voice.

"Leimomi Sanchez?" said Clarence quietly. "Leimomi Sanchez?"

"I'm crossing you in style . . ."

Clarence watched the woman on stage. His callused fingers tapped quarter notes on the bar. Leimomi walked slowly from one side of the stage to another, the wire to the microphone curled around her ring finger like a wedding band.

"Turn da TV back on," someone in the back screamed.

"Shaddup," said Leimomi. The piano player never missed a beat.

Fifteen years ago Leimomi Sanchez was the terror of Farrington High School, and the girl that Clarence Kalilikane loved. She was the biggest student on campus, male or female. The Bull of Kalihi, everyone called her. She cut in the lunch line, stole quarters, got suspended from school for harassing the varsity football team. She was a volleyball star, catcher on the softball team, center on the women's basketball team, outstanding female athlete of the year. Yes, Clarence loved Leimomi. Unfortunately, Leimomi did not give Clarence the time of day.

One night, after sitting on the bleachers of the gym watching Leimomi score thirty-eight points in a basketball game against the Pearl City Chargers, Clarence had worked up the courage to ask Leimomi out for a fruit punch.

"Uh, howzit, Leimomi," Clarence said as she walked out of the locker room. A towel was wrapped around her neck.

"What's up, Clancy?"

Her six-foot frame towered over Clarence's height at the time of five feet, two inches.

"Leimomi, I was wondering if, uh, if maybe you'd want to, uh, have a fruit punch with me?"

Leimomi laughed so hard her gym bag slipped out of her hand and fell onto Clarence's foot. Clarence limped home, soaked his big toe in ice water, closed all the curtains in his bedroom, and cried until he fell asleep.

"Thank you," said Leimomi. "Thank you very much. My next numbah is a favorite of mine. I hope it is one of yours."

Leimomi looked at the floor for a second and then brushed the hair out of her eyes. The piano player ran his fingers over the keyboard. "Feelings," sang Leimomi, "Nothing more dan feelings . . ."

"She's beautiful, huh?" said Clarence to Charley.

"Who? Leimomi?" Charley made a face like he had bitten into a very salty li hing mui. "Anyting you say, Coffinmaker."

After Leimomi finished singing, the television set was turned back on. Clarence's match with the Incredible Dagoo was in the third and final fall. Dagoo was on the ropes now, dazed by a Coffin-maker flying dropkick.

Clarence sipped at his beer and turned to Charley. "Tell me about dat Leimomi wahine," he said.

"She can sing okay," said Charley. "But she look like one man."

"What kind of ting is dat to say about a lady?"

"Ask her to show you her tattoos."

"I used to know her in high school."

"Jeez," said Charley, looking at Clarence's ears. "Dey really do look like cauliflowers!"

"Well, well, well . . ."

Clarence looked up. It was Leimomi. She was drinking a beer out of a long-necked bottle.

"Imagine running into you here, Clancy. You've grown since I last saw you."

"You looking good, Leimomi. I didn't know you could sing."

"It's a living." She cracked her knuckles. "So Ralphie at da bar tells me you some kind of big celebrity now."

Clarence smiled and looked at his beer.

"What are you?" said Leimomi, holding back a burp. "One actor?"

"No."

"One painter? One senator?"

"No, Leimomi. I'm a professional wrestler."

"I beg your pardon?"

"I wrestle. For money."

"You what? You pulling my leg, ah, Clancy . . ."

"And let me tell you, sweetie," said Charley Souza. "Da Coffin-maker, he's da best. Das him on da TV there."

"Da Coffee Maker," said Leimomi. "Now das a stupid name for a—"

"Leimomi," said Charley, "you don't know who you talking to. Da Coffinmaker here is da eighth wondah of da world, da master of—"

Leimomi turned to Clarence. "Didn't I beat you up behind da math building one time when you nevah let me copy your homework? Oh no. Try wait. Dat was somebody else."

"His body is one registered weapon with da FBI," said Charley. "And—"

"Professional wrestling," said Leimomi. "Everybody knows dat's *shibai*. Clarence, you little weasel, you couldn't hurt one cockaroach back in high school and you couldn't hurt one now."

"What a match we have here tonight," the television announcer was saying. "Ooooh, a body slam by the Coffinmaker! And another one! And, oh no, Dagoo has thrown salt in the Coffinmaker's eyes! What a dirty trick! He can't see, ladies and gentlemen! The Coffinmaker can't see . . ."

"Dis man here sent da Hollywood Sheikh to da hospital," said Charley. "Dis man here won da twenty-five-man battle royal at Aloha Stadium. Clarence Kalilikane is da Coffinmaker, and da Coffinmaker is da King of—"

"*Kākā.*"

A silence fell over the Blue Light Bar and Grill. The bartender nervously polished spots off wineglasses. On the television set Dagoo jumped off the top rope and put an elbow into Clarence's throat. "Ouch!" said the announcer. "Right in the Adam's apple. You could feel that one all the way to Kaka'ako, folks."

"You mean to tell me," said Leimomi, walking toward Clarence, "dat while I'm busting my butt singing four sets a night, six days a week to dese losers, you're oiling yourself up and wearing silly-looking tights and splattering ketchup on your face and making a million dollars a year . . ."

"I thought you were da prettiest girl at Farrington High School," said Clarence, trying to smile.

"I wanna take you on!" said Leimomi, pointing to Clarence. "Let's see what you got, Coffee Maker!"

"Leimomi," said Charley, holding up his hand, "da Coffinmaker is one professional." He turned to Clarence. "Go ahead, Coffinmaker. Show her da scar. Da one on your stomach from da forty-two stitches you got when Captain Dissection hid dat fork in his tights and went aftah you."

"Move da tables," said Leimomi.

And the patrons of the Blue Light Bar and Grill cleared away the tables. Leimomi took off her high-heel shoes. It was to be a one-fall match with a twenty-minute time limit. Money was passed between observers. Leimomi was a thirty-to-one long shot.

The match began. Leimomi and Clarence moved around in a circle. "Dis is too good to be true," said Charley Souza. "Tickets for da seat I've got would cost a fortune at da Blaisdell."

"Do it, Clarence," said someone sitting at the bar. "Give her da old Atomic Drop."

"I really should start heading home," said an embarrassed Clarence. "It's getting kinda late and . . ."

Leimomi charged Clarence and took his legs out from under him. Clarence fell to the ground.

"C'mon, Coffinmaker!" someone screamed. "Pile Driver! Give her da Pile Driver!"

"No, no," someone else said. "Abdominal Stretch!"

Leimomi went for the quick pin—somewhat of a mistake in professional wrestling circles—and Clarence lifted her off the ground and spun her above his head. It was the world-famous Coffinmaker Helicopter, which had ended the careers of Grizzly MacKenzie, Kamikaze Kawamura, and Werner von Skull, in that order. The men at the bar screamed, "Sleeper Hold, Coffinmaker! Give her da Sleeper Hold!"

Suddenly, though, Leimomi pulled at Clarence's hair. "Ouch," said Clarence, releasing his hold on Leimomi.

"All's fair, Coffee Maker," said Leimomi with a smile.

This went on for a good ten minutes. Once, Clarence had Leimomi in a half nelson. It looked like Clarence was a running back carrying a football, and Leimomi's head was the football. But Leimomi spun out of the hold, kicked Clarence in the shin, and put an arm bar on him. Clarence's arm was twisted behind his back. "Give up?" said Leimomi.

"You kidding?" said Clarence, trying to break the hold. "Do you know who I am? I am da Coffinmaker. You tink dat I'd—ouch!" Leimomi twisted harder. Clarence bit his lower lip.

"Give up, Coffee Maker?" said Leimomi.

"No."

Leimomi twisted even harder. The crowd at the Blue Light Bar and Grill gasped. Now Clarence's arm was at a ghastly angle. The knuckles on his right hand seemed to be pressed against the bottom of his left foot.

"Give up?" said Leimomi.

"Yes," said Clarence. "Ow! Ow! Yes! Now, let go of my arm!"

Leimomi released Clarence's arm and raised her own in victory. Silence. The crowd was stunned. Leimomi offered her hand to Clarence, and he shook it. Leimomi smiled and kissed him on the cheek. "Nice match, Coffee Maker."

"Call me Clarence," said Clarence.

"Okay. Clarence."

On the television set, Clarence and the Incredible Dagoo were slapping each other in the face. Suddenly, Clarence gave Dagoo a head butt and Dagoo fell to the mat. Clarence pinned Dagoo's shoulders down and one, two, three, the match was over.

"Uh, Leimomi," said Clarence, as he rubbed his arm and shoulder. "You wanna go out for a fruit punch?"

"You buying?"

"Yeah."

Leimomi fixed her hair, slipped her high-heel shoes back on her feet, and smiled.

"Let's go."

What the Ironwood Whispered

WHAT CAUSES A man to commit murder?

That's what I was thinking as I stood across from the hard, sturdy frame of Louis Kamaka—eye-to-eye—separated by the fading strip of white paint that represented the free-throw line on the basketball court at Lanakila Park. It had rained the night before and the asphalt was slippery and covered with puddles. Broken pieces of glass from beer bottles lay scattered around the pavement, and when the sun caught the glass at a certain angle, it sparkled strong enough to hurt my eyes. I watched Louis' massive chest go up and down, up and down in quick breaths. And then I looked into his eyes. Louis' eyeballs were large and yellow, and if I looked hard enough, I could see the red, tomato-colored corners where they disappeared into the firm bridge of his nose. Beads of perspiration fell into the lines of his forehead and ran down his cheeks like tears. It was his ball and the score was twenty to twenty. The last basket would win.

Louis dribbled the ball slowly and deliberately with his left hand, inches from his feet and his thin blue rubber slippers. I hand-checked him, putting my right hand on the damp white T-shirt that stuck to his sweaty back. He moved cautiously toward the basket and because of his strength, I found myself giving him room. He made a quick fake to his right and I bit. Then, palming the ball with his right hand as if he were doing a hook shot, he pivoted to the left, jumped high in the air, let out a savage yell, and slammed the ball into the basket. His hand banged against the loose rim, and the ball shot through the torn, dangling chain net with a metallic swish. Louis landed on top of my back and we tumbled to the ground, his arms wrapped around me to keep me from falling too hard. Particles of paint and dirt sprinkled down on us like rain from the still-vibrating backboard. My mouth tasted like dust.

"Whew," Louis said, wiping sweat from his brow. "You all right, or what?"

"Yeah," I said.

"Eh, dis game was too close for me," he said. "You getting bettah." Then he rose and helped me to my feet.

The stories I'd heard about Louis were the kind that stuck with you for a long time. When I was at Kalākaua Intermediate School, people said he killed a guy in a fight behind the bowling alley across from the Kam Shopping Center. Choked the guy to death with his own two hands. They said he took the body up to Kapālama Heights, cut it into pieces, and buried it under piles of fallen ironwood needles. I don't know if I believed the stories or not. I guess I didn't know Louis well enough to make up my mind. I didn't even know if Louis was aware of the stuff people were saying about him. But I do know one thing. Everyone seemed to know Louis' name. From the teachers in school to the cops to the minister at church. I even remember my mom telling me to stay away from him. Like I said, I don't know if I believed the stories about Louis or not, but whenever he scratched his elbow or tapped his fingers on the desk at school, I watched his hands—fascinated as hell—the way people might stand around in a museum looking at a gun that killed a lot of people. I tried to avoid him, but every now and then he'd call me to play a game of one-on-one basketball. Most of the time I told him I had something to do. But once in a while—like today—I lied to my mother and told her I was going to a friend's house to help paint his kitchen. Then I'd meet Louis somewhere. The last thing I wanted was for him to be mad at me.

"We go my house," said Louis, as we walked to the water fountain. "Still early, ah?"

"Yeah," I said.

"Good," he said. "Get someting for eat." He turned on the fountain and stuck his head under the stream of water. The water splashed on his face and spilled down the front of his shirt. Then he drank long, hard swallows. His Adam's apple moved quickly up and down. A little Hawaiian girl was jumping rope, and when she noticed Louis watching her, she smiled and jumped faster and began counting aloud. Louis shook his wet, shoulder-length hair like a dog, pulled it back over his ears, and took off his shirt. I walked to the fountain and drank. The water felt cool and crisp. The opening where the water came out was thick with dark-green moss and the drain was orange with what looked like rust. After I drank, we headed for Louis' house. The Hawaiian girl with the jump rope had disappeared.

Louis lived in a small wooden house on Pōhaku Street, a block or so away from the park. Across from Louis' house was the Kapālama Canal, a thin ribbon of water and mud and oil and algae and metal and anything else that fell into the rain gutters of Kalihi. The water, I guessed, came from somewhere in the rain forests of the Koʻolau Mountains and tapered down through Kapālama, winding past canneries and oil refineries until it spilled into Honolulu Harbor. Children from the nearby apartments often waded in the canal with their pants rolled up to the knees, slashing the shallow water with scoop nets and catching the small, striped tilapia and the slender, brown *medaka* by the hundreds. While they searched the beds of moss for more fish, they left the ones they had caught in plastic buckets to suffocate in the sun.

We turned into Louis' gravel driveway. An old man wearing glasses and a straw hat watered a hedgerow that lined the beige house. He wore a white undershirt and a gray pair of short pants. The old man's hair was well cropped and his gold-rimmed glasses sparkled like mirrors in the glare of the sun. A thick, musty-smelling pomade filled the air. He turned to us with a sudden, anxious movement, and asked, "Where's your mother?" The tops of his thin lips vibrated nervously when he spoke.

Louis looked at the old man. I watched Louis' long lashes and the yellowish eyeballs and the tomato corners near his nose. "You went sleep today, or what?" he said.

"Yes."

Louis took out the house key that was hidden at the bottom of an old shoebox.

"I bought fish," the old man added weakly.

"What?" said Louis.

"Fish. I bought fish."

Louis' mouth set firmly. "What kind fish?"

"*Ahi*. For sashimi."

"Sashimi? What da hell you tink? We rich or someting?"

"But—"

"Stupid." Louis opened the front door. The air in the house smelled musty, a mixture of varnish, old paint, wet blankets, and the ammonia-like smell of a catbox. When we walked on the floor, the wood creaked and the framed pictures of flowers and waterfalls that hung on the walls shook. Louis headed for the kitchen and I followed. A pot of rice lay in the center of the dining table. I could smell coffee and the stench of meat rotting in a milk carton near the sink. Louis opened the cupboard, took out two small plates and a wooden rice scoop, and walked to the table. There was a small brown cockroach the size of a raisin on the rice, and Louis swore and flicked it off with the back of his hand. The roach fell onto the wooden floor and ran into a stack of crumpled newspapers and magazines. Louis put the rice on the plates and opened the icebox. The bulb didn't work. He took out some milk and offered me some, even though there was only enough for one glass. I refused, but he insisted I take it. He then took out a pink Tupperware container filled with dark, greenish brown seaweed dipped in a *shoyu* sauce. The seaweed was fine, like thick hairs, and smelled of saltwater and vinegar. He picked up a pair of chopsticks and put a generous portion on both plates. "Picked 'em myself," he said.

"Where?"

"Kailua side."

"Haven't done dat in years . . ."

"*Limu* picking. Das one art dat stays with you forevah."

Louis sat down on an orange sofa and put his feet on the coffee table. Across from him was a small black-and-white television. The sofa was dusty, and when he sat it made a loud groan. There were colorful cushions on one side of the couch and a red futon on the other. Louis picked up a copy of the newspaper and looked at the television section. He rose and turned the set on to *Gilligan's Island*.

"I saw dis one," said Louis as he sat down. "Dis da one Gilligan gotta stay up all night and watch da orange seeds, but he fall asleep and dream about someting."

The front door opened and Louis stopped talking. The old man walked in, wiping his feet carefully on a mat. I noticed he walked with his back bent and his head down. He smiled and waved sheepishly and disappeared into the hallway. He closed a door and the walls shook. Louis shook his head. "Who's dat?" I asked.

"Who?"

"Da old man."

"Das my father." Outside, the crickets whirred.

Louis' father came back out. Now he wore an unbuttoned aloha shirt—blue with pink hibiscuses—and his hair was parted neatly to one side. In his right hand was a dark brown mandolin. The metal strings were copper with rust, and a thin layer of dust covered the polished wood. The old man was smiling.

"Put dat away," said Louis.

His father made a sad, disappointed face. His eyebrows sagged and he looked down at the instrument. He slowly sat down next to Louis and began to play. His thin fingers moved clumsily and hesitantly over the strings at first, but in a few seconds he picked up speed and began playing the opening strains of the "Hilo March" as if he'd played the mandolin all his life.

Louis watched the television.

"Where's your mother?" the old man asked Louis. Louis rose quickly and snapped off the television. He walked outside and slammed the door. I could hear the sparrows scream as they scattered off the telephone lines outside. I didn't look at the old man. I followed Louis outside and closed the door behind me.

He was in the garage, opening the door to his yellow pickup truck. There were shelves in the back of the garage filled with tools, plastic bottles of Prestone antifreeze, garden hoses, cardboard boxes with engine parts, WD-40, mousetraps, Armor-All, and a stack of worn-out tires. "We go smoke some *pakalolo*," said Louis, stroking his chin.

"Where?" I asked.

"Da old graveyard down da street."

"You crazy! My grandma stay buried in there. Besides, I ain't going smoke in no graveyard with dead people!"

"Nothing for be scared about," said Louis, looking away. "Dead is dead, brah."

Under the truck was a thick black pool of oil. Crabgrass and dust had accumulated in the puddle.

"We go beach, den," said Louis.

I got in the truck. The cab had a sickening smell, like somebody had stepped in dog crap and wiped their feet on the rug. Louis worked the stick shift and released the hand brake. In ten minutes we were cruising Koko Head–bound on the H-1 freeway. Ala Moana Beach is a popular place with locals because, if nothing else, it's convenient. I mean it's easy to get to, and it's like in the center of town. Over at the beach, there's a place called Magic Island where people gather by the hundreds to jog, toss Frisbees, barbecue, sunbathe, bicycle, fish, swim, and surf. I don't know what's so magic about the place but that's what they call it. To the left of Magic Island, if you're facing the ocean, is a sort of pool created by a stack of boulders that serves as a breakwater. Louis and I swam to these boulders. I was pissed off watching Louis and his steady, constant strokes, while I was left about fifteen yards behind, swallowing water and wondering how deep the water was and pumping hard with my legs, feeling the cramp welling in my calves. We climbed onto the rock wall and sat facing the horizon. The wind felt cool against my skin.

"Rob-boy," Louis asked, "you still working service station?"

"Yeah."

"Wish I had one job," he said, pinching his nose to remove the water. "But who da hell would hire me?"

"Maybe once you graduate, you find—"

"Ain't going graduate."

"What da hell you talking about?"

"Screw dat place. No ways I going back." A large wave slammed against the breakwater, and I heard the ocean sound rush under the boulders beneath us.

"Eh, brah," I said, "gotta graduate."

"I no need do nothing," said Louis. The wind was loud, and his voice sounded soft and distant. "I going play basketball. Be one millionaire with da Lakers."

"You crazy."

"Why?"

"Get planny guys who good, tink dey can play for da Lakers. Like da guy from Leilehua—Filipino guy—Bautista. And what about all da guys in New York and Chicago?"

"I scruff Bautista one-on-one."

"What if you no can play pro basketball?" I asked. "What if you ain't good enough?"

There was a long silence, and I felt bad about asking the question.

"Den you know what I going do? Hah?" Louis looked at me. He made a fist and the knuckles in his thick hand cracked. "You know da small pond behind da bar on School Street? Da nice pond dat dey lock up?"

I nodded.

"Get one catfish swimming around in there. Just one. Big, strong, and fast. I going catch da buggah. I promise I going catch 'em."

I hadn't been to the pond in years, but I remembered it as a very quiet and still place. The water was a dark green and the trees reflected off the placid surface. It was long, maybe seventy-five yards, but not very wide. It would take no trouble to throw a baseball from one side to the other. The water was cold as ice because it was fed by a small underground well. The strange thing about the pond was that as far as I knew, no one ever knew its name. It was just the pond with the catfish.

All the kids in Kalihi wanted to snag that catfish. I once had him, too. I was fishing for some large tilapia that I could sell to the old Filipino men, when something hit my line. The monofilament shot out of my reel and buzzed like a hundred dentist drills. I knew I had the catfish. I fought it for about ten minutes and I felt it tug and it was like holding a magnet in my hand in front of a large piece of metal. All of a sudden, the fish jumped out of the water and wriggled in the air. I saw the thick body and the long, long whiskers and the black, dead-looking eyes. It was only then, when I saw it curl in the air and shine in the sun, that I knew I really wanted it. I fought it for another ten minutes and then the slack of my line went dead. I knew that my bait, hook, and lead were gone.

———

MY BOSS, MR. OLIVEIRA, was a tall Hawaiian man with curly black hair and a tiny wart, the size of a small bread crumb, on the corner of his left eye. When he smiled you could see his teeth had become yellow from tobacco and coffee. He used to be a Kamehameha Schools fullback, and he always talked about the time he returned a kickoff seventy-eight yards for a touchdown in Honolulu Stadium. Not long ago he lost his wife in a car crash, and I only found out about it when I read it in the obituaries. "Why da hell da newspaper gotta print dat kine stuff?" he told me. "Dey should just leave us alone. We tell when we like tell."

I had worked for Mr. Oliveira a little more than a year. I met him last summer in a pool hall on Gulick Avenue. We got together and shot several rounds, and we got to talking about our favorite surfing spots and what kinds of cars we'd buy if we had the money. I beat him in three games, won fifteen bucks, and he offered me the job.

"Howzit, Robbie," he said as I came in to work. He was under the hood of an old model Toyota SR-5. The metallic blue color of the car was the shade of faded denim jeans. Mr. Oliveira's hands were big and strong, and the cords and muscles in his forearm twisted and danced when he turned a bolt with a wrench or loosened a screw. I walked over to him. He was sizing up the SR-5 for a new radiator. The grill was cracked and torn, and small flies and moths—white, as if frozen in ice—were lodged between the spaces in front of the radiator.

"Mr. Oliveira," I said, "I like ask you one question."

"Look dis baby," he said, gesturing toward the car. "How you figgah?" He smiled and scratched the back of his neck with the crescent wrench. I laughed.

"Uh," I started again. This time he looked at me. "I, uh, I know one guy who work hard and, uh, looking for one job."

"Friend of yours?" Mr. Oliveira wiped the oil off the crescent wrench with a towel. "Go same school as you?"

"Sort of."

"I know 'em?"

"Maybe."

"What da name?"

"Kamaka. Louis Kamaka."

He looked at me. There was a pencil stuck behind his ear. His brown eyes did not move, and I saw the beads of sweat in the pores of skin below his nose. "Louis Kamaka. Kamaka. I heard dat name someplace before . . ."

He wiped his fingers on the towel and patted my back. I walked outside, looked up the hill toward Kapālama Heights, and felt the wind in my hair. I imagined the breeze blowing around the fallen needles of the ironwood trees. I wondered if Louis would ever catch his fish.

————

IT WAS THE closest I ever got to running away from home.

I was fourteen and in the eighth grade and it was Halloween night. There were three of us—Keala, the oldest; Foster, the youngest; and me. It was about nine or so and we had finished trick-or-treating. Keala was still wearing his mask, a glow-in-the-dark Creature from the Black Lagoon. I had covered my face with a thick red liquid that they sold in drugstores that was supposed to look like blood. Foster went trick-or-treating without any mask. Keala said he didn't need one because he was ugly enough.

We were sitting down on the lanai at Keala's house. He lives in one of the low-income housing areas in Kalihi Valley. Keala was eating a Reese's Peanut Butter Cup, and I sucked on a lemon-flavored lollipop. In the parking lot, Keala's father buffed the fender of his Impala. The night was thick with quiet.

"One night we should go up there," said Keala, pointing with his finger toward the dark mountains. "Das where supposed to get da guy Louis went kill."

"What guy?" I asked. I think it was the first time I'd ever heard the story.

"You know da guy Louis Kamaka? Basketball dude?"

"Yeah."

"He went kill one guy. Right behind Kam Bowl."

"Nah," I said. "Why?"

"My father told me. He choked da guy's neck, cut da guy up, and buried 'em up Kapālama Heights."

"One of my friends knew one guy who found some bones up there," added Foster. He had a terrible scab on his knee from falling off his skateboard. He picked at the scab and some of the skin was green with pus. The black hairs near his knee curled and tangled in the softness of the raw skin.

"Why?" I asked. "Why he went kill da guy?"

"We go up now," said Keala, smiling and looking at me. "We go get one shovel and dig da guy up!"

"You crazy," I said. "My father would kick my ass if I went up there at night."

"No need tell 'em."

"No ways."

"Why?" he asked. "Scared?"

"No, but—"

"Panty."

"Where we going get da shovel? No more shovel."

"Your old man get one," said Keala. "I seen 'em."

"You nuts," I said. "My old man would kill me if—"

"Panty."

The first thing I always remember about that night up on the mountain was how dark it was. When I put Keala's flashlight against my palm, I could see the bones and veins—all orange—right through the skin. And when I aimed the flashlight into the ironwood trees, I saw the beam of light reach through the shadows like those spotlights the airport uses on dark nights. It was cold, and we kept warm by wearing two jackets each. Keala led the way with the flashlight. I felt secure being second.

There were no moon and no stars, and once we were up on the mountain, no one mentioned Louis or the body. The ironwood needles on the ground were wet and slippery. Foster carried my father's old shovel over his shoulder. No one said a word, but our footsteps were very, very loud. Keala was the first guy to stop. My heart was pounding in my chest and throat. "Pass da shovel," he said to Foster. Foster gave him the shovel and Keala started to dig. He was strong and didn't have much trouble breaking the soil. It had rained earlier and the ground was soft and damp. I could smell the dirt. Foster held the flashlight over the deepening hole. Several pill bugs ran out of the hole and scampered beneath the fallen ironwood needles.

"What if Louis watching us right now?" asked Foster in a whisper. "What if he getting ready for kill us?"

The air was getting colder. I didn't say a word. Keala dug deeper.

Somewhere down the valley, someone was chopping wood. I could hear the hollow thud of the axe, steady and hypnotic like the sound of an old clock.

"What da hell is dis?" asked Keala suddenly. Foster knelt and picked up a small white fragment, maybe an inch long. Keala aimed the flashlight at it and dusted it off with his finger.

"One bone!" said Foster.

"Bone, my ass," said Keala in a louder voice. "Das part of one tree." He threw the branch away and we moved to another spot deeper into the dark forest.

We walked for another ten minutes and the grade of the mountain got steeper. We had to grab hold of roots and vines to keep from falling off the sides. Foster was breathing heavily behind me. The spaces between the trees were pitch-black. Keala stopped and stood at the edge of a cliff. We looked at all the lights of the city and we saw the dark ocean. "Can see my house, or what?" asked Foster.

"Right there," said Keala. "By da freeway."

"Where's da freeway?"

"Dose row of lights. So bright, brah! Blind or wha—"

Silence. Keala looked at me. He'd heard it, too.

"What da hell was dat?" I asked.

We stood silent and heard the sound again. Footsteps in the grass.

"You heard 'em?" Keala asked.

I nodded.

We turned and scrambled down the mountain, falling and scraping our knees and arms and faces, tripping over each other's legs, snapping branches with loud cracks. All the while, Foster screamed behind us, "Was Louis! I saw Louis! He had one knife! Hurry up! He coming aftah us!"

I never learned what the hell those sounds were. Maybe a wild pig, or one of those mountain men who plant *pakalolo,* or the wind, or maybe just our damn imaginations. Imaginations, shit. The next day I got dirty lickings and was grounded for a week because I left dad's shovel up on the mountain to rust and be buried under the needles of the ironwood trees.

———

I HADN'T SEEN Louis for a couple of weeks, so I decided to walk over to his house and make sure everything was all right. Several

Filipino boys were playing Hawaiian-style football in the street. The main difference between Hawaiian- and American-style football is that with Hawaiian-style, you can throw the ball as many times as you want in any direction you want. I looked at the lawn and the mailbox and the house. A faucet against the wall dripped slowly, plopping water into a small puddle in the well-cut grass. Louis' pickup was in the garage. The fenders and windshield were covered with red dirt. Through the curtained plate-glass window of the house, I saw the black-and-white flickerings of the television set.

I walked up the steps and the wood creaked loudly. There was a small white doorbell but I knocked on the wall instead. The television went off and I heard footsteps through the house. The door opened. Louis had grown a thick beard. He stroked it and looked at me for a while as if he didn't recognize me. His eyes were very red. After a while, he invited me inside. The air was cool because a breeze was coming in through one of the open windows, but the catbox smell of ammonia still lingered heavy in the house. I heard the crickets chirping outside and the faucet below the window dripping. Inside, the icebox hummed monotonously. "What's up?" he said.

I sat down on the sofa. From a crack in one of the windows, I saw the mountains of Kapālama Heights and the tall ironwood trees.

"Just seeing how everyting's going," I said.

"Still alive." He sounded annoyed. He walked over to an embroidered flower design that was framed and hanging on the wall. "Nice, ah?" he asked, straightening it. "My mother did 'em."

"Yeah," I said. "Must take long time."

"How's school?" he asked.

"Still there," I said. "Miura like you come back. You can still graduate if you study up. He said you making one mistake." Miura was the school counselor. He was also Louis' basketball coach.

"Tell 'em I said no need school." Louis sat on the coffee table and picked up a forty-pound dumbbell and started doing curls with his right arm. The muscles in his forearm vibrated to the rhythms and clankings of the metal weights, and the veins in his bicep pressed insistently against the dark skin. His fingers looked thick and firm wrapped around the metal bar.

The sound of the mandolin came from the hallway. Louis placed the weights on the floor and the walls shook slightly. The music stopped and I heard the door open. I sat watching the afternoon sun high over the mountains. The air looked gray. The old man's shadow appeared from the hallway and fell upon a bookshelf filled with empty liquor bottles. Louis stood up, his fist clenched. I stood up also.

"Louis," said the old man gently, "did your mother buy groceries today? I told her to pick up some—"

"What I told you?" asked Louis.

"I . . ."

"I told you for fucking stay in your fucking room!" Louis was shouting. Then he punched the wall and the house shook. Several of the framed works of embroidery fell to the floor. "You deaf or what, you bastard?" He punched the wall again and the glass in the window rattled. The old man disappeared quietly, with his head down, into the hallway. Louis followed. I heard him say something. Then I heard him slam the door. Louis came back into the living room, his fingers twisted in his hair. He shook his head and sat down. I got up to leave.

The sound of the mandolin began again, this time more quiet and tentative.

———

SOMEONE HAD VOMITED outside the bathroom at the gas station over the weekend, and the smell coming through the Kona wind made me gag. I stood over the bucket hoping the Pine-Sol would drown out the bitter, sickening smell, but my stomach still turned uneasily as the mop smeared the brown, sand-colored puddle into a mess of chunks of orange like carrots and green like lettuce. Then, when I rinsed the mop in the bucket, the puke caught and dangled in the rope ends. I swore at the bastard who did it, whoever he was. I saw the empty case of Heinekens in the back of the garage and swept up the broken green bottles. I could tell someone had cracked the bottles by throwing them against the wall. The afternoon sun was directly over my head and I felt my shirt sticking to my back. I took out the bathroom key and opened the door. The floor was wet and slippery. The drain in the toilet had clogged with toilet paper and the water had overflowed. I swore and mopped my forehead with the back of my hand.

"Howzit," I heard. I turned around. Louis was eating a bag of *li hing mui*. It was a big bag—the expensive one that runs a couple of bucks—and I declined when he offered me some. "Hooo, what a mess. What da hell happened?" He carried a fishing pole, a small tackle box, and a plastic bag filled with what looked like bread crumbs.

"Somebody puked ovah here." I explained about the case of empty Heinekens in the back of the garage.

"Jeez," he said. "You know what you should do? Next time, hide. Den when da buggahs come again, nail 'um. Punch da lights out. Just hide. Like in da bushes or someting."

"Where you going?"

He smiled when I asked him.

"I going catch me dat damn fish."

————

I DON'T KNOW what made me go over to the pond that day after work, but I did. The fence was locked with a bicycle chain, but it wasn't very high and I climbed over. Once on the other side, I walked on the soft mondo grass and listened to the birds and the crickets and the occasional plop of a tilapia breaking the surface of the placid water. It was a shame nobody seemed to know the pond's name. For the longest time, I thought it was the most beautiful place in the world.

Louis, wearing a baseball cap, sat on the bank of the pond. He sucked on a blade of grass. Next to him was a small Hawaiian boy. Louis' hand was on the boy's head, and the boy's head rested on Louis' shoulder. The boy's smooth, sun-streaked hair looked reddish in the sun. Louis smiled when he saw me. I waved and walked over.

"Any luck?" I asked.

"Naw," he said. He had a small Garcia reel, the kind my father uses when he goes shore fishing for ʻōʻio or *weke* down the Waiʻanae coast. Louis' denim jeans were rolled halfway up his calves, and the curly black hairs on his legs were wet and stuck to his brown skin. The boy next to him played with a dark-red crayfish, teasing the legs and watching them paw at his finger.

I looked into the pond. There were three large rocks in the deepest part, right in the middle. The rocks were covered with moss. Occasionally sparrows and mynah birds sat on the rocks and picked at their feathers. I don't know how long we sat there, the three of us, talking about everything that came to mind: cars and beers and cartoons and cheerleaders. The sun started to sink behind the milk-white apartment houses. The laundry lines and television antennas stretched against the darkening sky like the silhouetted legs of large insects.

"Next week da big day, ah?" asked Louis, slowly reeling in his line.

"Yep," I said. "Just bought da cap and gown. So damn expensive and all you do is wear 'em once. My folks, dey pretty excited."

Louis smiled distantly. "Das good." He opened the plastic bag and rolled a small piece of bread into a ball between his thumb and index finger. Then he put the ball into his mouth and wet it. He fastened the moist ball of bread onto the hook and cast his line into the green belly of the pond, into the space between the three large boulders. That's the place I first hooked the catfish.

"What you going be doing from now on?" I asked Louis. I scratched my nose and thought I could still smell the vomit on my hand.

He pointed toward the pond. "I told you already. I going hook dis catfish."

"What happens aftah you catch 'em?"

There was a long silence. The boy let the crayfish go and it skittered into the shallow water and disappeared.

"Ask me when it happens."

———————

I'VE FORGOTTEN THE name of the small Hawaiian restaurant on King Street that always looks closed. It has red-framed windows and dirty-colored bricks, and smoke from the kitchen flows out through a smokestack on the roof. Behind the place is an apartment surrounded by laundry lines and dried shrubs. Old ladies from the apartment are always washing their clothes in the basin near the parking lot of the restaurant. The parking lot is unpaved and when you drive through it, dust flies everywhere and you have to roll up your windows. Louis called me the day before graduation and asked me to meet him at the Hawaiian place for lunch.

I got to the restaurant first. The air had a funny smell, strong and not very pleasant, like the smells of pork and dishwater and coconut and fried fish and cooking oil and crushed taro leaves. Ferns hung from straw baskets dangling from the ceiling. Every now and then, a hum came from the soda machine. It was lunchtime but I was the only person in the place. An old radio on the wall played Hawaiian music.

Louis came in fifteen minutes late and sat down. An old Portuguese lady came out with a notepad and Louis ordered *laulau,* poi, salmon, raw Maui onions, and two beers. He didn't even look at the menu. The waitress stuck the pen behind her ear and repeated the order. I wondered who the hell was going to pay for all of this. "Sorry I late," said Louis. There were patches of dirt beneath his thick fingernails.

"Das all right."

The beer and the onions came first. The lady placed two cocktail napkins on the table and set down the cold brown beer bottles. Louis told her that we wouldn't need the glasses and she nodded without smiling. Then she put down the Maui onions with a side order of Hawaiian salt. Maui onions are the sweetest in the world. We sprinkled the salt on them and ate them raw, like apples. Louis smiled and drank his beer. "Eat up, brah. Dis is my, what you call, graduation present to you."

"Present?" I asked. "Where da bucks coming from?"

"Nah mine," he said, making a face. "Just eat up. You always worrying about money."

The *laulau* came next. The steam from the taro leaves rose like ribbons into the ceiling fans of the warm restaurant. We started eating. The food was good. "So what, schoolboy?" he asked between bites. "What you going do now dat you graduating?"

"Work. Fix car . . ."

"Clean up vomit." I looked up. Louis smiled disarmingly. "Nah, brah. Take it easy. Only joking." He sipped his beer and laughed loudly.

"What about you?" I asked. "What you going do?"

"I get by."

"What you going do for cash?"

"No worry about me," he said, finishing his beer. "Planny money."

"You tink you can live off your parents forevah?"

Louis put the empty bottle down and began to peel off the wet label.

"My parents," he said quietly. "Shit."

————————

I'VE KNOWN LOUIS for a long time—at least I've known who he was for a long time. I think the first time I ever really met him was at basketball tryouts. We were both sophomores in high school, but he was already starting and averaging about ten points a game. The papers called him a dangerous player because he was very physical and moved quickly. When you played a zone and left him alone in the perimeter, he'd hurt you with his twenty-foot jump shot. When you played a man defense, he'd move you into the key and with his speed and aggressiveness, get into position for the lob or the dunk. Anyway, he was at tryouts, standing on the bleachers watching us— popping his gum and spinning a ball on his finger—while the rest of us grunted and sweated and swore and cried through sets of layups, wind sprints, five-on-fives, and rebound drills.

Once I played against Louis and he sent an elbow into my chest. I lost my breath and had to gasp for air. My eyes were open, but all I saw was blackness. A small Filipino boy named Antonio Domingo came over and helped me to my feet. "Das dee guy who went kill somebody," said Antonio. "He play dirty, yeah?"

I never made the team. I was cut in the last round. But I still went out and watched the games now and then. Louis was listed as a guard in the program, but because of his large, thick frame, he often played at forward. I remember a game against McKinley. Near the end of the game, with Farrington well in control, the McKinley guard drove down the floor on a fast break. Louis sprinted down-court and laid an elbow flush against the guy's head. The McKinley guy fell and his head hit the floor. The trainer had to come out with a towel and wipe up the blood. The crowd booed, even the Farrington guys.

The next day I was in the weight room doing bench presses. Louis was in the corner by himself doing squats. It was early afternoon, just before lunch, and the air had a dusty, yellowish color. Louis came up to me and asked if I had a cigarette. I told him no and he walked away. Three guys came into the weight room and asked me if I knew a guy named Louis. I pointed him out. They walked over to him, and when he saw them, he rose slowly to his feet. The three boys jumped him. One guy grabbed his throat, one guy grabbed his hands, and one guy tried to tackle his legs. Louis spun around, and with a loud scream, picked up a long, thick weight bar. He held it parallel to the ground like a spear, and screamed, "What? C'mon, you bastards! C'mon!" The three made a hesitant circle around Louis. One guy pulled a knife. Louis swung the bar and hit one of the guys square on the temple. It made a horrible, dull sound. The boy fell to the ground, bleeding from the ear. Once he was on the floor, he didn't move.

Louis watched the two other boys. "Who next?" he said quietly. "You tink you big with dat pole, ah?" said the larger of the two standing boys. He wore a gray sweatshirt and a headband.

"Put 'em down," said the boy with the knife. "No need weapon, brah."

Louis threw the bar down. It made a high-pitched sound that echoed in the hot, small room for a long time. Like a tuning fork.

"What now?" said Louis. "Outside, you bastards."

Both boys laughed, and the one with the knife charged Louis and stabbed him in the stomach. I didn't know what the hell was going on. Everything was moving in slow motion, like in a dream. A fucking bad dream. The blood spilled from the spaces between Louis' fingers. It was a dark color, almost black. Louis' yellow eyes were on fire and his teeth were set in a tight, trembling grimace. He tried to reach for the bar, but the boys ran out of the weight room. The dark blood was all over the concrete floor, and red splotches the size of raindrops fell like wet paint onto the benches and equipment.

Louis stepped over the third boy, who was still on the floor, and slowly grabbed a set of weights for support and gently set himself down on a bench. He put his head down and placed his hand on his stomach. He swore, and a thin ribbon of blood spilled out of the corners of his tight lips.

"I going call Mr. Ahuna," I said. Mr. Ahuna was one of the physical education teachers.

"Nah, brah," said Louis, standing up slowly. He tried to smile. "I all right."

And he left, just like that.

I watched Louis walk out of the dark room, and then I looked at the boy he'd hit with the bar. He was still lying on the floor. His hair was dark and sticky and wet, but it didn't look red. It was like he'd just gotten out of the shower. A custodian came in with a mop and bucket. He looked at the puddles of blood and the red fingerprints on the door and the weight machines and the benches. Then he looked at me.

"Damn you kids," he said, shaking his head. "Damn you no good kids."

———

"WHAT'S YOUR PROBLEM? You no like poi?"

I looked up. I was jabbing my spoon into the brown mound of poi in my bowl. "I do," I said, laughing.

"Hope so," replied Louis. "You Hawaiian, ah?" A pretty Chinese waitress came out of the kitchen and he ordered two more beers.

"Half Hawaiian," I said.

"What da othah half?" He gave me a piece of his *laulau* and said he wasn't very hungry.

"All kine. Portuguese, Japanese, little bit Filipino, some English . . ." I raised my knee and bumped the underneath of the table. Someone had stuck a piece of chewing gum there and it caught on my pants.

"So what?" asked Louis. "All your folks going be there tomorrow?"

"Yep," I said. "My old man going take pitchahs. My mother, she stay picking *maile* with my aunty from Kaua'i. My uncle bringing ovah couple cases of Budweiser."

"Lucky you get nice family."

I smiled. The Chinese girl brought the two beers and Louis gave her a five-dollar bill.

"Yep," said Louis, "you damn lucky."

———

MR. OLIVEIRA SAID that he would slap my head if I didn't take the graduation present he stuck in my hand. It was an old white envelope, and I opened it under the lightbulb that hung from a thin chain on the ceiling above his desk. In the envelope was a crisp twenty-dollar bill. "I knew you could do it," he said. "You get brains. You one good boy."

I smiled and he patted me on the back. "Now I can work real hard for you," I said. "I can learn how fix car and do da body work like how you wanted me for learn."

Mr. Oliveira was looking at me, running his hand through his hair. "I don't know," he said.

"Mr. Oliveira. You ain't going fire me, ah?"

He smiled and his grayish eyebrows sagged. "No, Rob-boy. No . . ."

I was relieved.

"I was just tinking, good boy like you, maybe you should get da skills for work someplace else. No waste your time dis kine place. Maybe learn electronics. Das where da money stay. Electronics."

"But I like learn how fix cars. I like it here. You one good teachah."

"You tink I like seeing you clean up vomit? Scrub toilets? You bettah den dat, Robbie."

"But—"

"You go out look for anothah job. Where dey can treat you bettah, like one man. Where you can make one name for yourself. Go where you can keep your hands clean and make planny money. If you no can find one place like dat, and you decide you really like fix car and get your hands all dirty and covered with oil, if you decide you like work twelve hours a day, take apart engines, den I'll be happy to have you back." Mr. Oliveira placed a large hand on my head and looked at me. I could see myself in his eyes. Behind him was an old *Playboy* magazine calendar and a row of boxing posters. "Dis is always your home," he said. "If you no can find anyting bettah, you can always come back."

I clutched the envelope in my hand and knew that whether I actually wound up with another job or not, the hardest thing in the world would be walking back into Mr. Oliveira's gas station.

———

GRADUATION DAY WAS a shower of color, and the air was thick with the smell of carnations, plumeria, roses, and pikake. Eight hundred of us—the largest senior class in the state—cloaked in maroon and white, walked two by two in straight, disciplined lines as the band under a canvas tent in the corner of the amphitheater played "Pomp and Circumstance" over and over and over again.

There was a light rain falling from the mountains, and I remember thinking, as the flutes trilled and the drums rolled and the cymbals crashed, about the many times in study hall and cafeteria lines and homeroom that I had wondered and dreamed about this moment.

I was in line with a guy named Ben Puahi. Puahi, or Puhi as we used to call him, was my oldest and best friend. We went all the way back to the days over at Kalihi Kai Elementary when we used to raise pigeons and go hunting for hammerhead sharks under the bridge at Sand Island. Puhi was a big dude. He was the catcher for the baseball team and batted three hundred, four years in a row. He was also the runner-up in the state wrestling championships. He lost in the finals against some Japanese guy from Pearl City who was a black belt in judo. The Pearl City guy swept Puhi's legs and then used a hip throw to slam him to the mat. Then the Japanese guy pinned him, all in less than a minute. When Puhi got up, he patted the Japanese guy on the behind and smiled. That's one thing about guys like Puhi. They know how to win and they know how to lose.

There was a large crowd standing behind the roped-off areas of the walkway. Mothers and fathers and big brothers and little sisters and calabash cousins were snapping photographs and thumbing through programs and pointing and clutching sweet-smelling plastic bags full of leis. I felt the smooth gown on my arms, and I fixed my cap nervously several times.

"Well, my man," said Puhi, "it's all ovah." It seemed strange to see him so well-shaven. All the boys stood tall with clean faces and newly cut hair. It was the damnedest thing.

"Yep," I said.

"No more waking up six-thirty in da morning. No more biology."

"Kind of sad, though."

Puhi looked around at the pink-colored buildings. "Yeah," he said, "I know what you mean."

I heard our names over the crackle of the loudspeakers. "Robert Kahoano and Benjamin Puahi." Puhi raised his hands in the air.

"Dis place get some memories," he said. "Remembah da game against Kaiser when I blasted da tree-run homer ovah da fence at Lanakila Park and da baseball went hit da bus?"

I smiled.

"Everyting going be different from now on," he added.

As we marched up the bleachers in straight lines, I thought about everyone in high school and what Mr. Oliveira had said yesterday, and I wondered what the hell we all would be doing, say, a year or two from now. Puhi waved at a girl and I smiled. She was a pretty Filipino girl and she wasn't wearing makeup. None of the girls wore any makeup. They didn't want their tears to smear it.

The band played the alma mater and then everyone sat down. The principal was introduced and he started to speak. I could hear the wind blowing over the microphone. From behind the bleachers where we sat, someone called my name. I turned around. It was my cousin Kewalo. Kewalo was rich as hell because he was manager of several fighting chickens and got large commissions off the cockfights. He even made the razor-sharp knives that were tied to the birds' feet. I smiled at Kewalo, and he held up a bottle of Jack Daniels.

Then to the right of him, I saw Louis. His yellow eyes caught mine and he held my glance, but he did not smile. He looked at me and slowly nodded his head.

After the principal finished talking and we were officially declared graduates of Farrington High School and everyone threw their caps in the air and firecrackers went off in the bathrooms, I turned to the spot where I had seen Louis standing next to my cousin, but he was gone.

———

AN OLD HAWAIIAN lady with her gray hair in a neat bun was picking mangoes off the tree in her yard. She had woven some stiff wire into a round cup—like a scoop net—and connected the cup to a long piece of bamboo. She stroked the branches of the large tree and caught the fruit in her net. The Filipino boys were playing football in front of Louis' house. I watched for a while as one boy ran deep, stumbled on a rock, and fell down. The ball landed on Louis' mailbox and bounced back into the street. I picked up the ball and threw it back to one of the boys. The boy who had fallen down saw me walking into Louis' driveway, and shouted, "He no stay home."

"Where he went?" I asked.

"I don't know," the boy said. His knee was bleeding and he limped back to the huddle. "Everytime nowadays, Louis no stay home."

"Where he go?"

But the boy didn't answer. He was in the huddle. Louis' truck wasn't in the garage and the curtains to the house were drawn tight. I turned around and left. They sent the boy with the bleeding leg deep again.

"Boy! Boy!" The old lady was calling me.

I turned around, smiled, and walked over. Her property was separated from Louis' by a scattered row of lichen-covered rocks. She had a laundry basket full of ripe common mangoes.

"You looking for Louis?" she asked.

"Yeah," I said.

"You one friend of his?"

I didn't answer.

"I no see da boy long time. All time he go out."

I thought about the bag of *li hing mui* and the twenty-dollar lunch. "Does he come home?" I asked.

"Night time he come," the old lady said. "Yell at da father."

"How come he yell at da father like dat?"

"Wha?"

"Da father. How come he yell at da father?"

"Louis?"

"Yeah."

"Da father *pupule*. Nuts. Da buggah crazy."

I looked at the shuttered windows.

"What you mean, *pupule*?" I asked.

"When Louis was one small boy, da father came home one day and caught da wife screwing around with anothah guy. Louis' father took out one hunting knife and chased da guy out. Den he went aftah da mother, but she came running into my house and I hid her."

"Jeez . . ."

"She no come back. Been years now. She ain't nevah coming back. Louis' father, da buggah went crazy. Talk to himself at night. Waiting for her. Sometimes I hear him crying and swearing. Give me da creeps. And all da time I hear dat mandolin. He play one mandolin, you know. So lonely sounding. I close da curtain and shut my ears. Long, long time ago, when he and Malia—das his wife's name, Malia—was in happier times, dey would sit outside with baby Louis and da old man would play his mandolin. Sometimes I feel sorry for Louis."

"But—"

"Da old man is good-for-nothing. Useless. *Pupule*."

I turned around to leave, and the lady asked me to take home some mangoes. I smiled and shook my head. The Filipino boys were still playing football, but the boy with the cut leg was nowhere to be seen.

———————

MOM INSISTED I go to the cemetery and drop off a carnation lei for Grandma and tell her that I graduated. Grandma died when I was in kindergarten. One thing I remember about Grandma was her squid luau. She taught me how to dry the squid and dip it in a bucket full of white garlic sauce until the legs curled. Another thing I remember about Grandma was the way her clothes smelled when she walked past me. She always smelled like aloe because she tore the plant and rubbed the sticky liquid on the burns she got on her arms from cooking, and on the blackened, rotten gums in her mouth. Now, once a year—usually near Easter when the ladies set up booths outside the cemetery and sell lilies—I visit Grandma and bring her a pot of flowers or a bottle of beer or a cigarette, and I sit down with her and talk out my problems.

It was early afternoon, but the graveyard was cool because it was shaded by tall, thick oleander and plumeria trees. I made my way through the heavy yellow brush—along the short barbed-wire fence—and found Grandma's stone. The tombstone was nothing more than a foot-high piece of cement, shaped something like a washboard, with Grandma's name, birthdate, and the day she died. It was caked with red dirt and sparrow crap. I kneeled down and placed the carnation lei on the dried grass around the stone.

How you doing, Grandma? I graduated yesterday. Now I going be one good boy. No need worry about me.

I felt the wind at my back. The birds were loud in the trees. Birds always sing loudest in cemeteries. That's what Dad always tells me.

I not going be missing school too much. I mean, I still going be playing basketball with Joe and Willie and Mario and Sammy. Maybe we go out shoot couple rounds of pool, go on Grant's boat, drink beer, and cast for papio.

I ran my fingers over the slug tracks on the headstone. The carnations still had a sweet, rich smell. Behind me I heard the dull sound of a shovel scratching soil.

You should've been at da graduation yesterday. With all da flowers and everyting. I marched with Puhi. Had some big bashes aftahs. Drank one whole bunch of Lowenbraus and tequilas. Drank da bottle and swallowed da worm. Got so wasted and fu—I winced. *Nah, Grandma, wasn't dat bad.*

A cardinal sat on the sharp edges of the barbed-wire fence.

Still working for Mr. Oliveira. But I don't know. He said dat da money stay in electronics. He like me make one name for myself. Electronics . . .

The sky was blue and there were no clouds over the ocean.

What does heaven look like, Grandma? Is it like in da books?

A line of red ants cut through a patch of withered blades of grass, carrying a long, dead gecko.

On weekends, maybe, I can go ovah to da pond and try snag da catfish. You know da one I always tell you about? Da one I had on my line dat one time? You would have been proud if I snatched dat dude. Was bigger den da ulua Dad caught da time he went Lāna'i. I extended my hands about a yard apart. *Nah . . . maybe not dat big . . . but lots of guys trying for snag da catfish. Get dis one guy, Louis. Remembah him? I told you about him. People say he killed one guy. I don't know how anybody would be able for do someting like dat.*

Kam Bowl was a block away from the graveyard and if I looked hard past the trees and the yellow flowers, I could see its white concrete walls.

Mom's all right. Still working at da delicatessen and complaining about her back. And Dad stay working on one house in Moanalua, by da airport. He said he might take us camping next month. I kinda remembah how you used to like to come camping with us. I remembah da time in Kaua'i when was real cold and you went lend me your sweater. Where was dat? Ha'ena side, ah?

I watched a white moth fly into the sky and disappear in the glare of the sun.

Someone tapped my shoulder gently and I turned around quickly. Louis smiled and tapped my cheeks. His forehead was smeared with dirt and his arms were caked to the elbows with mud. He was carrying an old rusted shovel made of metal that had been painted red. "Dis your grandma?" he asked.

"Yeah."

Louis squinted and cleaned the dirt off the headstone with his fingers. "She lived long . . ."

"Yeah."

"She was happy. I can tell."

I smiled. Louis wore denim jeans and a torn white T-shirt with the sleeves cut off. His big hands were wrapped around the handle of the shovel.

"What you doing here?" I asked.

"Dis my place," said Louis, spreading his arms. "I work here."

"Yeah?" I asked. "Since when?"

"Last week."

"No scared, or what?" I asked. "Work graveyard?" I remembered the stories people told me about the cemetery. Especially the one about the old man—a Korean who had two families and was blind in one eye—who sold bubble gum and cheesecake and ice cream and bowls of noodles in a small van parked alongside the cemetery. He worked late hours, and one night, people heard a scream and the sound of the windshield and windows of his van cracking, as if someone were throwing stones and shattering the thick glass. When they checked on him, they found the old man curled in his van, his eyes open wide in death, streaks of blood running parallel down his flesh and the white walls of the van. The slices on his chest were clean and precise, like claw marks. The cops burned the van in an empty lot on Sand Island. And in the graveyard, the grass never grows near the place where they found the body.

"Come," said Louis, putting his hand on my shoulder. "I like show you someting."

I followed. Louis, whistling an old Hawaiian song that always played on the radio, led me to a hole in the ground. The odor of damp soil filled the air—the smell of lichen and mold and dried root. It smelled like the mountains after a hard rain.

"Tell me da truth, Rob," said Louis, gesturing toward the pit. "Da ting straight, or what? One side look kinda crooked?"

"Uh . . ."

"Tell da truth. Dis my first job. Did 'em myself. What you tink? I should fix da edges, or what?" The hole was shaped like the nameless catfish pond, long but narrow. There was a mound of dirt in a neat pile next to the hole. On the dirt were cubes of cut grass. I looked deep into the pit. The dirt was rich and brown. "Nobody went help me with dis buggah. Did 'em myself."

"Uh, looks okay, I guess," I said, trying to smile.

Louis stared at the hole and closed one eye. "You sure not lopsided?"

He took me by the arm again. His fingers were hard and callused. We walked through the thick yellow grass with the smell of blooming plumeria sweet and milky through the air. I stepped cautiously, not wanting to walk on any of the markers. Louis wore his thin blue rubber slippers. I read the names on the headstones. Many were Hawaiian, with inscriptions and oval, black-and-white photographs of grandmothers and wives and husbands and fathers and little children. I wondered who took all the pictures and what happened to all of the people and their sons and daughters.

"Nothing for be scared about," said Louis. "Everybody gotta die. Das da least ting for worry about. Da least ting." He bent down and emptied a vase full of dead flowers. Then he poured the putrid-smelling water into the dried soil and tossed the flowers into an empty trash can. The smell of the old gray flowers was as bad as the dark-colored water.

We reached a small wooden shed with a corrugated roof. Louis opened the combination lock and we walked in. Inside was a chair, a table, and a small basin. On the table was a transistor radio and a thermos. "Dis my office," said Louis. "My place. Aftah I walk around and cut da grass and trim da hedges, I come in here and sit down and tink." Louis was nodding. The air smelled of sawdust, rust, and coffee. Louis placed the shovel against the wall, next to an old manual lawn mower, broom and dustpan, hoe, handtruck, and a wheelbarrow half-filled with gravel. "Dis whole yard. It's my responsibility. Louis Kamaka's place. Rob-boy, you see what I'm saying? Dis is my place."

He smiled and looked at the corrugated roof of the shed. Then he picked up the shovel and we walked outside. The sun was bright. I followed Louis as we wound our way through the cemetery. I could see the muscles in his shoulders and back moving up and down, up and down.

"But what you going do for da rest of your life?" I asked.

"What you mean?"

"You cannot go digging graves for da rest of your life . . ."

Sweat ran down his armpits and onto the mud on his chest and forearms. He squinted as he looked at me. "Why?"

"Nobody dig graves for their whole life," I said. I couldn't explain.

"What dey do?" said Louis.

I paused. "Maybe electronics, or someting. Where you can make one name for yourself."

Louis shook his head. "But I happy here. With da shed and da soil and da worms . . ."

"You crazy."

"What da hell you talking about?"

"I mean . . . you young . . ."

"I no can dig graves? Is dat what you trying for tell me?"

"Not for da rest of your life."

"Den you know what I going do?" said Louis, after a while. "I going wait for you at da catfish pond."

"Wha?"

"Das what I going do. I going wait for you at da pond."

He stuck the rusted shovel into the dirt, and its shadow and Louis' stooped back pointed directly toward the ironwood trees swaying gently in the breeze high on Kapālama Heights.

The Day Mr. Kaahunui Rebuilt My Old Man's Fence

EVERY TIME IT rains, I think about the place.

There was a house overlooking my backyard with dirty white walls and a green roof with peeling asphalt shingles. The plumbing hummed loudly in the middle of the night, and the screens were torn, as if by large, angry cats. When planes flew over the house, the chipped and dried paint fell to the ground and collected in the patches of mondo grass that sprouted through the cracks in the concrete driveway. If you had seen the house, you might have told yourself that it looked a little run-down but was still a steal at sixty dollars a month. But let me tell you, bad things—terrible things— happened in there. My grandmother kept asking us how we could live next door to an evil, unhappy house like that. She wanted us to move to Liliha, near the bakery, and live with her.

Many years ago, Dad started building a fence between our house and the house overlooking our backyard. I was just a kid. It was on a winter day near Christmas. Three days later, Dad got a call from the merchant marine, and the next thing I knew, he was packing his bags and leaving on an evening plane for Singapore. I never saw him again. He left Mom, my older brother, Kirk, and me out in the cold, scrounging for rent money. Mom worked twelve-hour days at minimum wage just to put food on the table. The unfinished fence grew soft and moldy, an eyesore that no one had the time to finish up or take down. But Mom seemed to like it there. I guess she thought that as long as the fence was up, it was like Dad was home. Or coming home.

Bad things kept happening in the house overlooking our backyard, but a funny thing happened as I grew older. It was like I got numb—immune—to the questions from the ladies in the grocery lines, the visits from the priests, the newspaper write-ups, the people moving in and quickly moving out. Even the damned violence.

It was only after living next to the house for almost twenty years that I finally learned my lesson. It was a bad place, just like the old ladies said—an evil place. When Kelly Ahuna, a girl I went to high school with, moved into that house, it concerned the hell out of me. But I tried to tell myself that Kelly was a smart girl, a strong girl, and if anyone could live in that cursed house and break its spell, it was her. I sure as hell was wrong. This is not a ghost story. But I'll never let anyone I care about near that evil house again.

———

MR. KAAHUNUI HAD no telephone, so I caught the number-one bus to his place in Kaimukī. I hadn't seen him in years. Everyone on the bus seemed to be reading the newspaper. Kelly's picture, the one she had taken for her high school graduation, was on the front page. Mr. Kaahunui lived above Pak's Groceries, and children eating shave ice and ice cream sat on stained wooden benches outside the old store. I knocked on the screen door of his apartment, and Mr. Kaahunui pulled back a thin white curtain and unlatched the door.

Mr. Kaahunui was a big man, about six-four and maybe three hundred pounds. He looked bigger in person than he did in his pictures in Dad's old programs and magazines. Mr. Kaahunui used to be a professional wrestler. My old man and Mr. Kaahunui went back a long way. He was the best man at Dad's wedding. Mr. Kaahunui was nearly bald now and shaved his head very close to the scalp. One cauliflower ear was almost closed, and Dad said Mr. Kaahunui was blind in one eye. There were triangular-shaped scars on his cheeks and forehead. Those came from the screwdrivers and broken-necked beer bottles wrestlers used to hide in their trunks and boots. Dad was always talking about a match Mr. Kaahunui had in the Civic Auditorium with a guy named the Hollywood Sheikh or something. They were locked in an enormous steel cage, and a chain was tied from one of Mr. Kaahunui's wrists to the Sheikh's. Dad said there was blood all over the place, and Mr. Kaahunui won when he grabbed the Sheikh by the hair and began rubbing his face back and forth, back and forth against the iron bars of the cage. Dad said the Sheikh's nose was hanging from his face like tinsel from a Christmas tree.

"Long time no see," said Mr. Kaahunui. "Whoo, you big boy, now."

Mr. Kaahunui's voice was soft and very hoarse. A wrestler named Mad Man Kobayashi broke his windpipe by jumping off the top rope of the ring and landing with his knee in Mr. Kaahunui's throat.

"You looking like your old man now," he said as I walked in. There was a smell of burned cooking oil. "For a second there, I thought was your daddy standing outside."

I was a bit flattered because from what I could remember, my old man was a pretty good-looking guy.

Mr. Kaahunui sat at the kitchen table, wearing reading glasses and feeding a Siamese fighting fish he kept in an old jelly jar. I told him I hoped I wasn't bothering him and he said no, no, he always welcomed guests. We talked for a while, mostly about my dad, and then I asked him if he'd help me finish Dad's fence. He looked at me funny, glanced through the television guide, then shrugged and offered me a ride home.

When we got to my house, Mr. Kaahunui looked at the fence and shook his head. The fence—speckled with brown gecko crap the size of rice grains—was now crooked and covered with brittle crusts of lichen. He ran his thick fingers over the wood and it splintered under his touch, like rust on the sides of an old automobile.

"How long dis buggah been here?" he asked.

"Ten years, come Christmas."

Mr. Kaahunui let out a whistle and smiled. "Ten years, ah?" Dad always called Mr. Kaahunui "Smiley" because Mr. Kaahunui was always smiling and had the nicest, straightest white teeth. And when Mr. Kaahunui smiled, there were dimples in his cheeks as big as cherries. "Dat long, ah? Seems like only yesterday your old man and me was shooting pool and raising hell down on Hotel Street."

"Dad started dis fence when I was a small kid," I said. "Da year he went away."

"Jeez, da last time I seen you, you was dragging one blanket around with you every place you went. Like da kid in da comics. What da buggah's name?"

"Linus."

"There you go. Das it. Linus. Eh, you big boy now. How many years school you get left?"

"Me, I one senior now."

Mr. Kaahunui grabbed the top of the fence and shook it. The dirt beneath the fence caked and gave under the movement of the wood. "Gotta tear da whole ting down and start all ovah again," he said, shaking his head.

"But we can finish 'em, right?" I said. "You and me?"

"Oh yeah," Mr. Kaahunui said. "Too bad your father no stay around, though. He was one damn good carpenter. Me, all I know how for do is eat and sleep."

"And wrestle."

"No, no. Mr. Kaahunui forget how wrestle."

"Screw."

"Mr. Kaahunui forget dat, too." He smiled, and I wondered how a guy who used to fight in iron cages could have such straight, white teeth. "Yes suh, too bad your pop no stay. Singapore, hell. He could rebuild dis fence in one day. Me, I don't know how fix stuff. Only know how break. Brokanic."

"Make da fence high. I no evah like see da damn house again."

Mr. Kaahunui looked up into the sky and squinted. "As long as no rain," he said.

"We gotta build da fence," I said, looking up at the sky, too. Thick, dark clouds covered the sun, making it look like a dust ball. "Dat house is no good."

"Always I heard stuffs about dis place," said Mr. Kaahunui. "But you know me, I no believe nothing. Not unless I see 'em." He took out a crushed pack of Kools from his back pocket and lit a cigarette. He started to cough and he sounded like an old man with bad lungs.

"I finally learned my lesson," I said.

"No worry," Mr. Kaahunui said, smiling. "We get da job done."

"Mr. Kaahunui," I said, after a while, "I should have told Kelly."

"Wha?"

"Long time ago, I killed one guy in there." I said it real quick and real quiet.

"Hah?" said Mr. Kaahunui, smiling. "No mumble, pal. Us old men, we no hear too good. Whatchoo said?"

"Nothing," I said, relieved. "Nothing."

I REMEMBER THE day Dad started the fence. I'd just turned seven. We collected all the wood he had lying around the yard and underneath the house.

"Are we gonna make da fence high?" I asked. "Like at Honolulu Stadium?"

"Not dat high, boy."

"What da fence for, Dad?"

"Keep da stray cats out of da yard."

"Kirk says dat house is no good. Is da house haunted like Kirk says?"

"Whatchoo going be, kid, when you grow up? One professah?"

"Somebody went die in there?"

Dad smiled and rubbed his fingers on his chin. "It's your mother. She no like da house. She all time complaining dat when she do da laundry and she gotta look at da place, she get all nervous. It's either build da fence or move da laundry lines." The lines swayed over my head, and the shadows stretched across the yard, marking mango trees and ceramic pots and fertilizer bags.

"Do you hate da house, Dad?"

"House is a house. How can you hate one house?"

Mr. Kamitaki walked up the driveway carrying a mop and bucket. He was the owner of the house, an old Japanese man who stooped over when he walked and filled the air with the smell of Wildroot hair oil. He smiled at me and I smiled back and Dad asked about his fishing and Mr. Kamitaki said the *ulua* were biting like hell past Portlock. Then he took a key from his pocket and opened the screen door of the house. It was the only time I would ever see the inside of the place. Everything was still. There were just the walls and the hardwood floors. The house was empty.

"How come people always move out of your house, Mr. Kamitaki?" I asked.

He smiled and ran his hand through his hair. His hair was generally dark, but there were long streaks of gray curling like corkscrews across the top of his head.

"I don't know, boy," he said. "People always moving."

"Maybe get ghosts," I said. "My brother, Kirk, says people die in your house."

"Boy!" said Dad sternly. "Shut up awready. Let Mr. Kamitaki do his work."

"Kirk said da house get ghosts dat make da walls bleed."

"No," said Mr. Kamitaki, smiling. "No more ghosts." He put his hand on my head. "If I thought people could get hurt in my house, I'd burn dis baby down with my own two hands." He snapped his fingers. "Just like dat."

"No more ghosts?" I said.

"No more ghosts, boy," he said. "Only get cockroach."

Dad laughed. Mr. Kamitaki walked into the house, and I could hear him laughing in the kitchen, complaining about the cockroaches.

————

THERE WAS AN old man with a dark face and white hair down to his shoulders that I saw every day, sleeping under overpasses and coconut trees, standing alongside traffic lights and watching the signals change. He wore either a baggy gray shirt or a black polyester aloha shirt. On hot days, if he wore the polyester shirt, you could smell him a block away. No one knew his name or where he came from, but he waved every time he saw me.

One day the old man was sitting on the steps of my house. I was in the seventh grade at Kalākaua Intermediate School and coming home from after-school practice with my Polynesian music class. I played the vibes and acoustic bass. The corners of the old man's left eye were twitching, and a small vein pulsed through one thick gray eyebrow. "Going rain tonight," he said.

I looked at the sky. It was clear.

"Tonight," he said. "Big rain."

"So?" I said.

"I sick." He coughed softly, then harder and harder, until he cleared his throat loudly and spit out a dark, hard ball of mucus and blood. It seemed to beat like a heart on the surface of the hot sidewalk. "Lemme sleep in your house," he said. "Just for tonight. Till da rain pass."

"Ain't going rain tonight." I looked up at the clear sky one more time.

"Please . . ." He began to cry. He fell on his knees and wrapped his arms around my legs. I could feel the stubble of his chin through my pants. "Da rain going kill me, boy . . ."

"Ain't going rain, old man."

It rained hard that night, but I forgot about the old man. I sat in bed, reading a Batman comic book and listening to the rain pound the corrugated metal over the garage. Kirk had invited over some of his friends on the football team, and they sat on the lanai drinking cheap wine and blasting Hawaiian music on their portable radio. I got out of bed and went outside.

The four of them wore long-sleeved sweatshirts and shorts and sat around a hibachi. The charcoal was still hot, and now and then, when the wind blew, it burned a dull orange. One of the boys, Jeff, sat on a big plastic cooler playing his guitar and trying to keep up with the Sunday Mānoa music.

"So I was in da back seat with Leesa," said Ben, a defensive back, " and I went tell her—"

"Eh!" said Jeff, smiling and winking at me. "Da kid! Give da man a seat!"

"So what about dis Leesa?" said Kirk.

"Nah, not in front da kid, brah," said Ben. "X-rated. No one undah eighteen admitted . . ."

Kirk pulled up an old Wesson oil can and I sat on it. Jeff was still trying to play the Sunday Mānoa. The others passed around a large, three-dollar bottle of burgundy. The fire from the hibachi felt nice with the rain falling hard around us. The breeze began to pick up, and you could smell the faintly sweet, acid smell of the insecticide from the house next door. The house was covered with a large, yellowish brown plastic tent and a red sign with a skull and cross-bones that read DANGER! POISON GAS. When the wind blew through the tent, it made a whipping sound. The rain made a *tap-tap-tap* noise against Dad's unfinished fence.

I fell asleep, and when I woke to the rain on my face, I thought Kirk or one of his friends was spilling wine on me or taking a leak on me or something. But Kirk and his boys were asleep on the floor of the lanai. It was morning, and the sparrows and mynah birds sang loudly in the mango trees. The men from the exterminator company were removing the clothespins that held together the tent over the house next door. The smell of the insecticide was heavy in the air.

I was rinsing my face in the basin where Mom does the laundry when I heard the ambulance's tires crush the gravel in the driveway. There were no sirens or flashing lights. Two men dressed in white moved slowly and took out a stretcher. The ambulance driver asked the men removing the tent if it was okay to go into the house, and one of the men on the roof nodded. Kirk and his friends woke up. The dew on the mondo grass sparkled in the morning sun like diamonds.

The men in white came out of the house quickly. A white sheet covered a body on a stretcher.

"What da hell happened?" asked Kirk.

"Guy must've snuck inside last night," said the ambulance driver, shaking his head. "Clothes all wet. Nevah like get caught in da rain, I guess."

"No can read, or what?" said one of the exterminator guys as he took off the red warning sign.

"Happened before," said the ambulance driver, shrugging and spitting on the driveway just below Dad's fence. "Going happen again."

Mr. Kamitaki stood in the middle of a small crowd that had gathered. He pinched the skin between his eyes with his thumb and forefinger. The ambulance driver said something to him, then helped load the stretcher into the ambulance. Mr. Kamitaki looked at the house for a very long time. Then he closed his eyes, looked at the ground, and shook his head. His mouth was moving, as if he was trying to say something.

The cold water ran down my face. My knees were shaking, and I could hardly stand on my feet. I heard the old man's voice in my head, asking me if he could stay at our house for just one night. I had killed someone. Why the hell did it have to rain?

Kirk called the house a bastard.

————

AS WE PULLED out the planks from Dad's old fence, Mr. Kaahunui was saying that he wasn't as young as he used to be. He used the claw end of the hammer to tear out the nails. Then he grabbed the old wood with two hands and yanked it out of the soil. Sweat spilled down his head and fell onto the ground. It felt strange seeing Dad's fence lying scattered on the ground after it had stood in the yard for ten years—nothing more now than a bunch of old, termite-eaten boards. Mr. Kaahunui was breathing heavily, and the sound of the air coming out of his nostrils was like whistling.

"So how's your mom doing?" he asked. "Still one waitress? How's her back? She was always complaining about her back. Pretty lady like dat. I always thought she should've been one actress. *Hawaii Five-0* or someting."

"Mr. Kaahunui," I said. "I gotta thank you for coming ovah and helping me with da fence."

"Forget it, boy," said Mr. Kaahunui.

I placed all of the scattered planks into a neat pile. Then I looked at the porch of the house next door, and something caught my eye. Right where Kelly used to keep her slippers, umbrella, and jogging shoes, someone had left a single long-stemmed rose.

"Old bastard like me," said Mr. Kaahunui, scratching a mosquito bite on the inside of his forearm, near his elbow. "Nothing bettah for do anyway . . ."

"No scratch your arm like dat," I said. "Bumbye da buggah bleed."

"Good bleed," said Mr. Kaahunui. "Den no itchy."

No one said anything for a while. Mr. Kaahunui coughed and covered his mouth with a fist.

"Mr. Kaahunui," I said, "you seen dis morning's paper? Kelly's pitchah made da front page. You seen 'em?"

"I seen 'em," Mr. Kaahunui said. "Pretty girl."

"If dis house was a man," I said, "I'd cut his fricking throat."

"I don't know," said Mr. Kaahunui. "Maybe dey should come dig up da house. See what get undahneath. Maybe get some unsettled bones undah there."

I picked up a block of wood the size of a brick and threw it hard at the house. It hit the wall with a thud, right near the front steps, and then fell to the ground.

"Boy," said Mr. Kaahunui, putting his hand on my arm, "dat ain't going solve nothing."

"She was a good girl."

"Tings happen, boy. Nowadays, everyting happen so fast. In one day, tings can change, boom, just like dat. Even to nice people, bad tings happen."

"Why?"

"Cannot always ask why," he said. "You ain't always going find answers."

I shook my head and looked at the house.

"Da Ahuna girl?" Mr. Kaahunui asked softly. "She, uh, went your school, I hear?"

"Kelly? Yeah."

"Close friends?"

"Pretty much."

———

KELLY AHUNA WAS the most beautiful girl in the world. What made her seem even more beautiful to me was the fact that she didn't seem to know it. She lived with her grandmother in a small apartment near Punchbowl because her father was in jail and her mother had died of a heart attack. Kelly worked in a small beauty salon in Nuʻuanu, near Foster Gardens and all the mortuaries. I met her in a home economics class in high school. We were supposed to be baking a chicken, but I didn't know how to cut it, so she cut it for me. We started going to the library and then to dinners and movies. She was a year older than me, and she took me to her senior prom.

We were sitting on a park bench at Kapiʻolani Park one summer afternoon, watching children play soccer and people fly kites with long tails, when Kelly opened her purse and showed me a letter. She had gotten into the University of Hawaiʻi.

"Congratulations," I said.

Kelly's cheeks turned red, and she smiled and said, "And that's not all." She took out a folded piece of newspaper. It was the real-estate section of the Sunday classified ads. She showed me two house-listings circled in red. One was in Kapahulu, near Leonard's Bakery, going for a hundred and twenty dollars a month. The other was the house overlooking my yard.

"Take da Kapahulu house," I said. "It sounds like a bettah deal."

"Why?" she said, pretending to pout. "Don't you want me living next to you? The house next door to yours has three bedrooms for sixty dollars a month."

I had a hard time explaining to her about the house because I didn't want to scare her, so I watered down the facts, and the stories wound up sounding funny. All they did was make her laugh and play with her hair and call me names.

"I'm telling you, Kelly," I said, "I can't let you near dat place."

"Don't be silly," she said. "Listen to yourself. You sound like a seven-year-old."

"I just don't want to see you get hurt," I said. "Kelly, jeez, I care a hell of a lot about you. You don't want to live in there."

"But don't you see," she said, her brown eyes sparkling, "it'll be great. We could get two cans and connect them with string and talk to each other all night. Just like in the movies."

I had to smile.

"Before Dad left for Singapore and all, he worked his ass off trying to finish da fence in da backyard." She'd seen the fence before. I shifted on the park bench. "Bad tings happen in dat house. Evah since I can remembah. Evil tings."

"You're scaring me."

"Don't be scared," I said, putting my hand on her smooth arm. "The landlord didn't say there was anything wrong with the house."

That hit me like a rock. "Mr. Kamitaki?" It occurred to me that I hadn't seen the old man in years.

"Kamitaki?" she said. "The landlord is a guy named Nishioka."

THE AIR WAS getting so thick that even in the shade of the mango tree, it was still hot. I opened an old mayonnaise jar full of Dad's nails. In the corner of the yard was a rusty wheelbarrow with chipped red paint that Dad used to remove stones and bricks. I handed the nails to Mr. Kaahunui, and he bit down on each one, placing some into his pocket and throwing others on the ground.

"What evah happened to your brothah, Kirk?" he said.

"Kirk, he move out. Long time ago. Living Wai'anae now. Truck driver. Married and everyting. Nice girl from Kaua'i. Kid and all."

"I no can pitchah Kirk as one daddy," said Mr. Kaahunui. "What, boy or girl?"

"Girl. Tiffany."

"Remembah how he used to hate girls?" Mr. Kaahunui laughed and shook his head. "Seem like only yestahday I was rolling around with dat boy on da grass, teaching him how for wrestle." Mr. Kaahunui smiled. He really did have dimples big as cherries, just like Dad said. He wiped his forehead with the back of his hand. "Kirk married, I'll be damned. Next ting I know, you going get married."

I tried to smile.

"What da hell is dat?" asked Mr. Kaahunui suddenly.

"What?"

Under the shade of one of our large ti-leaf plants was a white object—like a large egg, only bigger—half-buried in the grass and dirt. I walked to the plant and dug at the soil with my hands. There was a silver trail on the dirt, left behind by slugs. I felt the dirt collecting under my fingernails, which I hadn't cut in a long time. After a while, I unearthed an old baseball. I scraped off the dirt that had caked on it. If I looked hard enough, I could still see the signatures of Dad's former teammates.

———————

DAD USED TO be a professional baseball player. He played Triple-A ball with the Hawai'i Islanders. Two or three times a week, Kirk and I would watch him practice or we'd go to the games at the Honolulu Stadium in Mo'ili'ili and watch him pitch. One day Kirk brought our baseball to practice, and Dad asked all his teammates to sign it. The threads of the ball were coming off and the skin was brown with dirt and mud, so the players had to press down hard with their dark ball-point pens.

Kirk and I used to throw the ball in the backyard after school. Kirk had an old third baseman's glove and I used Dad's pitcher's glove. Kirk threw the ball hard and it landed in my glove with a loud *pop* that rang in my ears. I had to catch the ball. I didn't want the thing in my face. Dad said that once he was hit in the mouth by a line drive and it took seventeen stitches to close the hole in his lip.

We were throwing the ball one day while Dad worked on the fence. I remember asking Kirk why Dad was building the fence. Dad was cutting boards over two wooden sawhorses.

"Because da house no good," said Kirk. "Haunted." I looked at the house. Someone was drying their clothes on the windowsill. The air smelled like strong detergent and dog crap. "Blood come out of da walls. Every time, da cops gotta come and mop da place and wipe da windows. Blood. I seen 'em."

"Not!"

"Yes!"

He threw the ball at me, but I turned my wrist the wrong way and it hit my arm and rolled to a stop at the legs of one of the saw-horses. Dad picked up the ball and tossed it underhand to me.

"Everybody who live in there, dey die," Kirk said. "Da place was built on one graveyard. Das why da walls bleed."

"Mr. Kamitaki said no more ghosts. Only get cockroach."

"You calling me one liar?" Kirk stopped throwing the ball.

"No."

"You bettah not," he said. "'Fore I kick your ass!" He whipped the ball at me and it bounced off my glove and hit a part of the fence Dad had just put up.

"Eh!" Dad said in a low voice. "Knock it off."

"You live in there," Kirk whispered to me, "you one dead man."

I looked at the house and at the plants Dad had pulled out to make room for the fence. I wondered if he'd finish before nightfall.

————————

IT WASN'T UNTIL she had spent about three or four months in the house that Kelly started getting upset because I was always thinking of something I had to do every time she invited me over. It was either work or the yard or the plumbing or maybe even something stupid like homework.

Kelly made a lot of friends in college. She was going to be a psychology major, she said, and maybe go into social work. Once or twice she invited her friends over for a party. I remember lying in bed, listening to the carefree laughter and the Hawaiian music. Once in a while, I'd peek outside and see her walking around with a tray full of grinds, wearing a pink dress and a yellow hibiscus behind her ear. I could smell the charcoal on the barbecue, and the fresh beer. The moon made everyone's skin look pale and silver.

One Saturday we sat in a small downtown restaurant near Fort Street Mall. Kelly was buying me lunch because I had gone with her to Kress to buy curtains. She'd fallen in love with these orange ones with tiny embroidered flowers. When she asked me to help her put the curtains up, I told her I was sorry but I couldn't.

"What's wrong with you?" she said suddenly. "You won't visit me. You didn't help me move my furniture in. What's wrong with you?"

"I can't go into dat house," I said. "I just can't. I'm sorry."

"Are you trying to tell me the house is haunted?"

"No," I said, "it ain't haunted, not with ghosts and stuff. It's just dat, jeez, bad tings happen in there. People get hurt. It's an evil place."

"Look," said Kelly, "I've been in that house for, what, four months now and nothing strange has happened."

"But see, Kel," I said, "das how da house works." I wasn't going to get into any arguments about how short a time four months was, because she was a student at the university now and was always talking facts and logic and all that other b.s. "All I know is people get hurt in there."

"Who? Who gets hurt? Do you know of anyone who ever got hurt in there?"

"Yeah," I said quietly, "I do."

"Who?"

"Kelly," I said, "there's so many stories I could tell you. One night, one rainy night, dey put up one termite tent. Had dis old dude—"

"I don't know why you're trying to scare me," she said, biting the fingernail of her pinky. "Do you know what it's like living in a one-room apartment with your eighty-four-year-old grandma?"

"I know what you're—"

"There aren't even any roaches or termites in the house," she said. "But it could use some repainting. We could go to City Mill and buy some paints and, *ooh*, brushes, and overalls . . ."

"How's da locks?" I said. "Old house like dat, people can just come in da middle of da night, when you sleeping, open da lock easy."

"Stop it!" said Kelly. "Stop talking like this!"

Kelly put her face in her hands, real quick-like, and I watched the light sparkle off the gold bracelet I had given her for Valentine's Day. I waited for her to look up, but she didn't. I hoped that she wasn't crying, but I knew she was. The restaurant was dark and there were ferns hanging in plastic pots from the ceiling. I heard the rattle of dishes and running water from the kitchen. I didn't know what to say, so I didn't say anything for the rest of the afternoon.

––––––––––

MR. KAAHUNUI HAD nails between his teeth, and he made a sucking sound with his mouth, like people trying to clean their teeth with a toothpick. He was on one knee sizing up wood with a tape measure. In his back pocket was a hammer. He wiped his nose with the back of his hand. A dog barked somewhere in the distance. Mr. Kaahunui smiled, and I hoped that when I got to be his age, I'd have teeth that white.

"You and my dad went back a long ways, ah?" I said.

"I used to go to da stadium, watch him pitch. He came down to da arena to watch me wrestle. Your father was always asking me, 'Eh, real or what, wrasslin'? Das real blood, or what?' I would be bleeding from my forehead aftah some stupid bastard bang my head open with one chair, or I would show him da bite marks on my arm, but still your old man would be drinking Seagram's with me, and asking, 'Das not real, ah? Das bull, ah?' Your old man. Always asking questions."

Mr. Kaahunui laughed and his eyebrows sagged. He stuck a large finger in his curled-up ear and looked at the sun. His face was a bit red. "Lemme show you someting," he said, lifting up a pant leg. His calf was discolored. "I still no more feeling ovah here aftah Killah Kamana came aftah me with one ironing board one night at da Civic. He went knock da referee out cold with one crescent wrench. Dey had to take da referee out of da ring on one stretchah. Killah Kamana, dat bastard. He stay on TV, making tire commercials now."

I looked at the leg. Mr. Kaahunui closed his eyes and told me to tap it. I put down the baseball we had found under the ti-leaf plant and tapped his leg, and he didn't open his eyes. He didn't believe me when I told him I had tapped it, so he told me to do it again.

"I was tinking about donating my body to science when I die, but I no tink dey going take 'em." Mr. Kaahunui laughed to himself. "Das da price you gotta pay for living one violent history, I guess."

"Wha?"

"Das what some reporter guy wrote about me in da newspaper.

About my, whatchoo call, wrasslin' career. Had one pitchah of me. Werewolf Collins was rubbing rock salt in my eyes, and there was blood all ovah da place—wasn't a good pitchah of me—and underneath, da caption said, 'A Violent History.' "

I looked at the wrestler with the triangular scars on his forehead and the dimples big as cherries. His left eye twitched every now and then, and when he stopped to rub it, the eyeball got very, very red. He patted his stomach and his belly shook.

"Yes suh," he said. "Das me. One violent history."

Mr. Kaahunui picked up the ball with all the signatures of Dad's teammates, turned it around slowly, and smiled. The old baseball looked very small in his hands.

"Your old man could pitch," said Mr. Kaahunui. "Da slider. Da fork ball. Da curve. Ninety-five-mile-an-hour fastball." He let out a whistle. "One night he struck out twenty-two batters. I thought for sure he was going to da majors. Just nevah work out, though. So he joined da merchant marine. Pissed your mother off."

"Yeah?"

"Oh yeah," said Mr. Kaahunui, picking at his teeth with his ring finger. He wore a large jade ring with a gold band. "She took it hard. But your father, he one hardheaded bastard. No can stay one place. Da most hardheaded bastard I evah met."

I looked at the house. A large green horsefly with a loud buzz circled the burned-out porch light, and a warm breeze rustled the bright-orange curtains that Kelly and I had bought at Kress. They were still hanging in her bedroom window, as if nothing had happened.

"Wish I'd met Kelly," said Mr. Kaahunui quietly. "Sounds like one nice girl."

I tried to laugh. "She would have loved you. All dose wrestling stories."

"Let's finish your old man's fence," he said, smiling. "Before da rain comes."

———

THE DALLAS COWBOYS were playing the Minnesota Vikings. It was a Monday night game, and the Cowboys were behind by two touchdowns. I was in the ninth grade and I had a big test the next day. Kirk and several of his friends were sitting around, drinking Millers and nibbling on *tako poke*. One of the guys, Ricardo, had speared the squid off Swanzy Beach, on the windward side of the island. This other dude, Jerome, was supposed to bring over some *sashimi* and poker chips, but he hadn't shown up yet. He was always like that. I had ten bucks on the Cowboys.

"Five more says Dallas scores here," I said.

Ricardo laughed. "Shoots."

Loud voices came from the house out back. A man's deep voice was calling someone a dirty bitch, and the other voice, a lady's, was crying.

"Radical, ah, your neighbors?" said another guy, Major.

"Always like dat," said Kirk. I was a bit embarrassed.

"Dey always fighting . . ." I stopped. It was first-and-ten on the Viking fifteen.

"Where da hell is dat bastard Jerome?" Kirk asked. "How we going play poker without chips?"

I heard the sound of pots banging the walls and glass smashing. Major laughed and turned up the volume on the set. We heard a slap and then loud crying. The man and the woman swore at each other. Then we heard a loud noise, a *pop*, like a firecracker or a car back-firing.

"You heard dat?" said Major. "Sounded like one gunshot."

"No ways," said Kirk.

"Maybe das Jerome's bug," I said. "You know his scrap-heap car."

"I heard 'em, too," said Ricardo. "Sounded like came from da house in back. Da haunted house. Maybe we should check 'em out."

"Shut up and watch da game," said Kirk. It was first-and-goal at the five.

"Eh," said Major, "dat sounded like one gun."

"Gun, my ass."

"Fricking Jerome. He bettah show . . ."

A knock came at the door.

I looked at Kirk and he looked at me, and then he looked at the floor and I got up and opened the door. My heart was beating fast. An old Hawaiian lady, her white hair hanging over her eyes, stood in the doorway. The moon bathed her in a silvery light. A few strands of hair were caught between her pale, cracked lips. She was crying, and mascara ran down her cheeks like black tears. She wore a string of pearls and an orange mu'umu'u. She looked as though she was ready to go out. I swear I didn't notice anything until Ricardo stood up and said, "Oh, God!"

Kirk rose and turned on the porch light. The lady fixed her hair and made a thin red smear on her forehead. She was barefoot, and her feet were covered with blood. She was trying to say something, but her mouth shook and she made no sound. I saw her red footprints leading to the doorway. The night was very, very cold. Slowly, she raised her hand into the light, and I saw the silver nail polish on her sharp fingernails. Her fingers were covered with blood. Clenched in her left hand was a black pistol.

———————

THE AIR HAS a funny smell just before it rains.

And you better believe that every time it rains, I think of that old man who died in the termite tent. Hell, I didn't think it was going to rain that night. Maybe if I'd had the guts to tell Kelly the story about the termite man, all of this crap would never have happened.

"Stop daydreaming and hand me dat board ovah by da plant," said Mr. Kaahunui.

I picked up the heavy board and passed it to him.

Mom never talked about Dad, neither did Kirk, but every now and then Dad wrote a letter, and we knew where he was by the name of the country on the stamp. We never wrote to him because his return address was always changing. Sometimes he didn't even write one on the envelope. I remember the last time I talked with him. It was the morning of the day he left—just three days after he had started the fence. He was clean-shaven and had cut his hair. He was working on the fence.

"Whatchoo going do when you go away?" I asked. Dad knelt on one leg, marking the wood with chalk. The smell of the wood was very sweet.

"Go on a boat and see different places," he said. Dad had a tattoo of a snake on his right forearm. When he wiggled his fingers, the lines in his forearm danced and made the snake dance, too. When I grew up, I wanted a tattoo like Dad's.

"Dad? What's wrong with da house?"

"I suppose you ain't evah going quit until you get one answer," he said, sighing. "All I know is evah since I can remembah, all kind stuffs happen in there."

"What kind stuffs?"

"I don't know," he said, putting his hand on my head. "I no can undahstand da place. But I tell you one ting. Dis house, da buggah is sharp, clevah. Someting bad happen and everybody, dey start talking, 'Eh, stay away from dat place.' So da place stay empty couple months and tings stay quiet, but aftah a while, people forget and somebody move in and *bang*, da whole ting starts all ovah again."

A pair of sparrows sat on the telephone lines above the house.

"You gonna come back and finish da fence, Dad?"

"Yeah," he said. "When I come back home, I'll finish it up."

He began pounding nails into the solid fence. I walked into the house and saw Mom packing Dad's bags. Next to the olive-colored duffel bag was a stack of blank envelopes.

—————

THE RAIN CAME very quickly. The sound was loud, like the roll of marching drums, and the water splashed out of drain pipes and spilled down the narrow concrete stairways. Mr. Kaahunui put his large hand on the top of the fence and shook it, but the wood and the soil beneath did not budge.

"Not bad for one old man wrestler, ah?" he said.

I smiled. "Maybe we should just do what Mom says," I said.

"What's dat?"

"Pour gasoline on da house and watch da bastard burn to da ground."

Mr. Kaahunui started hammering the nails into the fence. The rain began to fall harder and harder, and the cars on the road made sounds like tearing paper on the slippery streets. "Let's go in my house," I said, picking up Dad's old tool chest and his mayonnaise jar full of nails. "Take a break."

"I almost finish," said Mr. Kaahunui, squinting because the rain was getting into his eyes.

"Let's wait for da rain to settle down. Before you catch cold."

When we were inside, I made coffee and Mr. Kaahunui drank it black.

"I haven't been in here since da day your old man and your mom got married," said Mr. Kaahunui, sitting down on an old orange chair. "I was your dad's best man, you know."

"What was da wedding like?" I asked.

"Lot of baseball playahs and wrasslers."

"I've seen Mom's pitchahs."

"Wasn't she da prettiest ting?"

"Yeah." The air in the room was warm and still.

"Your dad stood right here, in da middle of da floor, and made one big speech about how there was no way in da world he was evah gonna leave your mother's side." Mr. Kaahunui smiled and shook his head.

"Mr. Kaahunui, you tink Dad'll evah come back home?"

"Das kinda hard to say," he said, smiling. "But you can nevah tell."

"You know what I no can undahstand?" I said, after a while. "If dis kind terrible tings happen to nice people like Kelly—people who was always trying to do good—what da hell kind world we living in?"

"I don't know, boy," he said. He ran a thick finger over his eyebrow and his voice became soft. "If da world can make one big, strong, dumb bastard like Mr. Kaahunui stay awake at nights and start tinking, you know dat someting very wrong, someting very bad is going on."

"Mom like move away from da house," I said. "She say she cannot take it anymore. She cannot sleep. But hell, we no more no place else for go."

"You fellahs can always stay with Mr. Kaahunui."

"Nah, we'd get in your way."

"No be stupid," said Mr. Kaahunui. "Always get room for friends."

"Thanks, Mr. Kaahunui," I said. "Thanks for everyting."

Mr. Kaahunui smiled. I listened to the rain and thought about the termite man. I wondered if that old bastard was pissed off at me, wherever he was. Then I began thinking about the house overlooking my backyard and who was going to move in there next. A lot of people could forget the stories in the newspaper for a roof over their heads at sixty dollars a month. Then I started thinking about Kelly and that afternoon at Kapiʻolani Park when she said that the best thing in the world would be the nights when we could attach a piece of string between two tin cans and talk to each other about silly things until the night became morning. The grayish light from outside came through the window and fell on the triangular scars on Mr. Kaahunui's cheeks and forehead. I thought the rain would never end.

The Three-and-a-Half-Hour Christmas Party

THE ONLY REASON Isaac Kalama went to the party in the first place was because he had heard that Sheila Awai was going to be there. Sheila Awai was a professional tennis player. Born in Mānoa —the same month and year as Isaac, as a matter of fact—she began doing the circuit at neighbor island resorts and rooftops at the age of nine. In her high school years at Punahou, she won all kinds of awards: girls' first in singles, most inspirational player, outstanding athlete of the year. *Sports Illustrated* ran a four-page article and a picture of her in a lei and a bathing suit, lying on the breakwater off Waikīkī Beach after she won a major tournament in New York City. Turned down scholarship offers from UCLA, Stanford, and Florida and played for the University of Hawai'i—because she'd die without the beaches, she said in *Honolulu* magazine. Isaac watched her on the news and heard her radio ads for everything from Bank of Hawaii and Taco Bell to sunscreen and hair conditioner. She took pledges on Labor Day telethons, played the piano for hospital patients, signed autographs at shoe stores. When Mrs. Kelly, a lady Isaac really didn't know very well, invited him to her Christmas party in Hawai'i Kai—where she promised, confidentially, the appearance of numerous celebrities and politicians—he wasn't really too keen on going. But when she mentioned that Sheila Awai was going to attend, hell, he just had to be there.

The last time he'd seen Sheila was five years back at, of all places, the Safeway produce section in the Mānoa Marketplace. That was around Christmas, too. Sheila and Christmas, they just seemed to go together.

––––––

IT STARTED OFF like any other ordinary day. Isaac had come from a softball game wearing shorts, slippers, and an old T-shirt he got for donating blood. The air in the supermarket was cool and smelled of cardboard, cellophane, and something like pistachio nuts as he wheeled his shopping cart past pyramids of canned soup and cartons of cheap wine. The loose wheels on his cart squeaked like mice on the smooth floor. In his pocket were coupons ripped out of the Sunday newspaper: fifty cents off frozen pizza; a quarter off mustard; buy one roast turkey TV dinner, get the second at half price. Two plays from the softball game were fresh in his mind. One was hitting a three-run homer in the third inning and the other was muffing a pop fly in the sixth.

And just like that, there she was—Sheila Awai—standing next to an old Filipino lady and squeezing tomatoes. Sheila said something and the woman covered her mouth and giggled. Isaac wheeled his shopping cart over next to Sheila. She wore a blue warm-up jacket with stripes running down from her shoulders to her wrists, white shorts, and *kamaboko* slippers. Her hair had a mild, sweet fragrance, like baby powder. She squeezed the tomatoes and put maybe nine out of ten back into the cardboard box. The supermarket's invisible speakers played Christmas carols. *We wish you a Merry Christmas, we wish you a Merry Christmas . . .*

Isaac tore off a plastic bag, picked out a tomato, and threw it in. He never bought tomatoes. In fact, he hated them.

"Oh, you don't want that one," said Sheila.

"I don't?"

"Oh, no." She made a face. "You want the firm ones. The ones that don't give. See?" She squeezed one. "Like this." She put the tomato in Isaac's plastic bag. Then she smiled.

We wish you a Merry Christmas and a Happy New Year!

Sheila Awai looked like a model on a fashion magazine cover. A girl who received all the right invitations, who knew how to nod, tilt her head, smile, wink. The kind of girl who'd turn your head and then ruin your day because you'd realize she was the kind of girl you could never get close to. A touch of rouge on already pink, high cheekbones. Eyeliner thin, dark, and intricate. Sheila's brown hair fell in gentle, disciplined waves over her shoulder, curling slightly as if an hour ago she had been standing in the rain. She moved with the grace of a cat, or better yet, a reef fish—a *manini* or a *hinalea*—nibbling at coral and swaying with the current. Yet there was something fragile, awkward about her. No, awkward's not the right word. Mischievous, impish, playful, childlike. Isaac didn't know. Whatever that characteristic is that certain people have that allows them to squeeze tomatoes with the enthusiasm of a cheerleader.

Her color was fair, almost pale. She had lost her tan in subzero hotel-room winters in Duluth, Milwaukee, Chicago, D.C., and Ann Arbor. Her arms were thin, deceptively fragile looking. No one would believe that the power to serve a tennis ball a hundred miles an hour lay in those forearms. And her legs—long and firm—looked like they belonged more on a Broadway chorus girl than a tennis pro. If you didn't know who she was, Sheila Awai could have been anybody: beauty queen, uptown model, Hollywood prima donna, East Coast debutante. But for some strange reason, she didn't seem to know it. And that seemed to make all the difference. The only thing that could have given her away were her fingernails. They were bitten short, all the way to the skin.

Isaac picked up another tomato. Sheila grabbed it and smiled. "That's a good one." He dropped the tomato into the plastic bag and wondered what he was going to do with all this fruit.

"Sheila? My name is Isaac Kalama. I don't know if you'll remember, but I interviewed you once. Many years ago. I was a sportswriter for the Farrington High School newspaper. You were playing in a tennis tournament at our campus."

"I remember," said Sheila, smiling. "We talked by the tennis courts. It rained a little. It was around Christmas. You wrote a nice article about me. I still have it somewhere."

"You do?"

Sheila placed her tomatoes on the scale. The Filipino lady picked out some garlic and said good-bye. Sheila smiled and waved.

"Listen," she said, smiling. " 'White Christmas.' "

"What?" Isaac said.

"The music. 'White Christmas.' One of my favorites. *I'm dreaming of a white Christmas, just like the ones I used to know.*' " She sang along quietly with the violins over the loudspeakers. "You know," she said. "I keep on thinking. What if it snowed one Christmas in Honolulu? Just once. Wouldn't that be great? Can you see it? I can! Snowman-building contest at Kapiʻolani Park? Ice-skating on the Ala Wai? Skiing down Tantalus?"

They took their groceries and stood in the express lane of the checkout counter. Sheila bought a handful of magazines. She didn't even look at the covers, just seemed to pick the ones with the most color, the most life. Then she picked up a Certs and a couple of chocolate bars from the candy rack. The checkout lady rang them up and wished them a nice day.

"Thank you," said Sheila. "Merry Christmas."

———

ISAAC LEFT HIS house an hour after Mrs. Kelly's party was supposed to start because he figured being the first guy at one of these fancy Hawai'i Kai parties was the ultimate embarrassment, a social no-no. Like walking into a classy restaurant with your fly down. He crossed the bridge into Hawai'i Kai where kids occasionally hooked nurse sharks. Yachts bobbed up and down in the marina. The drive from Kalihi Valley, where Isaac lived, to Hawai'i Kai could be surprisingly quick—twenty minutes if there's no traffic. Just hop on the freeway, which eventually becomes Kalaniana'ole Highway somewhere past Kahala Mall and the place where the old haunted drive-in theater used to be. Twenty minutes. Yet there's a world of difference between the two places. Even the sounds change. In Kalihi Valley you hear sirens and cocks crowing and helicopters looking for *pakalolo* or some escaped convict. In Hawai'i Kai you hear sprinklers.

Isaac was excited as hell. It had been five years since he'd last seen Sheila Awai—that day near Christmas, at Safeway—and he'd thought about her every day since. The way she walked, the way she talked, the way she smiled. As he drove, he sang along with every song that came on the radio, something he hadn't done in years. He wondered if Sheila was already at Mrs. Kelly's house. Maybe she had heard he was coming and was waiting for him. Maybe she was just as anxious as he was. Maybe the moon would fall out of the sky.

At every red light, he checked the street signs with the address he had written down on a matchbook cover. A road map was folded on his lap. Isaac was lousy with directions. He was the kind of guy who gets a hot dog at the drive-in movies and forgets where the car is parked.

The closer he got to the house, the more messed up he felt. This Hawai'i Kai deal was a long way from the drinking parties he was used to in patios and garages. The kind of thing where you came in shorts and an old loose shirt with more holes in it than a whiffle ball and stayed up all night on folding chairs with a guitar. Tonight he was supposed to be at a poker game at David's house. David had won big money on a football game and had splurged on foreign beer, the kind in green bottles. When Isaac told him he couldn't make it because he was going to see Sheila Awai tonight, David laughed, and said, "Yeah, yeah, nice try Kalama—you're a comedian—and while you're at it, why don't you wish for a million dollars."

Mrs. Kelly's house was a big three-story deal, way, way up in the mountains, with coconut trees, birdbaths, a swimming pool, and stone pagodas on a lawn that looked as big as a golf course. A mucus-colored Mercedes and some other foreign job Isaac had never seen before were parked in the three-car garage. After taking a deep breath—like a basketball player about to shoot the biggest free throw of his life—Isaac walked up the long, sloping driveway and rang the doorbell. It didn't go *bing-bong* like most people's doorbells. This one sounded like a symphony.

Isaac swore the door was as big as the door to a bank vault. He had no business at a party like this. Maybe he was underdressed, should have put on a tie. Maybe he'd spill gravy on the carpet, knock over a vase. He had splashed on some aftershave he got as a free sample in the mail. Maybe he had put on too much. Maybe it was too strong.

"Merry Christmas, Isaac," Mrs. Kelly said, opening the door. "You're early. Come in."

He followed her into the house. Mrs. Kelly—Mrs. Lucinda Kelly—was the kind of lady you saw walking a poodle at some Thomas Square dog show, or making a point to meet as many people as possible during intermission at the Diamond Head Theatre. She walked like a hen, taking small steps with her chest puffed out. She was in her late fifties, early sixties, with bags under her eyes that she tried to conceal with foundation and facial powder. She wore a long green dress, the color of pool-table felt, and her white hair was pulled back in a neat bun. To be honest, Isaac hardly even knew Mrs. Kelly. She was just some lady he met on the Pali Highway. She had a flat and it was raining like a sonuvabitch, so Isaac stopped and changed her tire. She thanked him and said something about saving her life and insisted that he come over to her house the following Saturday for a big Christmas party.

"I'm so glad you could come, Isaac," Mrs. Kelly said. "Would you like some eggnog?"

"Uh, do you have beer?".

Mrs. Kelly gave him a beer and a cocktail napkin and disappeared into the kitchen. Her house had the color of exquisite rust. The carpets were a dark gold, and the walls—covered with watercolors of docks, windmills, and European fishing villages—were varnished to a smooth, brown finish. The only time he saw houses like this was in decorating magazines lying around the dentist's office. The place was enormous. And everything was in place. You didn't want to touch anything. It was like having a party in an art museum.

Two girls sat at the piano, fingering through sheet music and inventing chords. One wore a backless dress, and when she laughed, her shoulder blades and the line of her spine pressed against her smooth skin. Isaac usually couldn't tell one song from another, but he knew they were playing a Christmas song because he had heard it on television the other night. The phone rang at least once every five minutes and when it did, everyone turned toward it like they were all waiting for an important call. Mrs. Kelly would answer, then call out a name that sounded vaguely familiar. Names with suave, catchy rings that you thought you knew but just couldn't place. Isaac looked at his watch and then turned toward the door and waited for Sheila. Five years. He wondered if she'd even remember him.

AN OLD, TIRED-LOOKING woman stood in front of a red kettle, ringing a bell for the Salvation Army. The bell made a loud noise that stayed in your head for a long time. The automatic supermarket door was out of whack, so Sheila held it open by leaning against it with her back. Sheila gave the woman a dollar and she smiled and said, "Thank you, ma'am." In the parking lot you could buy Christmas trees from big Matson trailers. Fathers carried the trees over their shoulders to their cars. The whole area was covered with pine needles. Isaac wheeled Sheila's groceries to her car, a white Corvette.

"Nice car," Isaac said as Sheila fished in her purse for her keys.

"You like it?" She opened the door, and Isaac placed her groceries into the backseat. Not an easy job, considering the backseat was full of tote bags, tennis rackets, shoes, socks, canisters of tennis balls—yellow, orange, even purple—headbands, and wristbands. "It's not really my car." Isaac figured, *Uh-oh, here it comes.* Probably belonged to her boyfriend, some stud actor or Scandinavian tennis star. "Well," said Sheila, smiling and running her hands through her hair. "I guess it's my car, sorta. See, General Motors sponsors this tournament and they let some of the players use the car for a year. I lost the tournament but they loaned me the car anyway. It's a pretty good car. Fun to drive. Hey, do you wanna go for a ride? Catch up on old times?"

"Yeah," said Isaac, smiling. "Sure."

And just like that, he hopped onto the sheepskin-covered bucket seat of Sheila Awai's Corvette. It was the strangest feeling, like being thrown into a new world in less than a second. Like when he dived for lobsters. One minute you're sitting on the boat, feeling it sway, feeling the sun, the damp coolness of the wood, listening to the water ripple. The next minute you jump off the boat and you're in a totally new world—underwater—where everything is green and murky, where everything moves slowly except the fish, where there is no sound except bubbles. That's how it was getting into Sheila Awai's Corvette.

Her car had a sort of organized neatness. There were no newspapers on the floor, no cigarette burns in the upholstery. The air smelled like sweet perfume. A teddy bear holding a tennis racket dangled from the rearview mirror. Sheila put on a pair of dark glasses and then fastened her seat belt. She turned on the radio and fiddled with the dial. The sound came through large speakers in the door. "There must be a radio station playing Christmas music somewhere. Ah, here's one." *City sidewalks, busy sidewalks, dressed in holiday style.* She turned the ignition and pumped the gas pedal and began to sing quietly. Isaac thought she really had a nice voice. She sang on key and knew all the right words and everything. *In the air there's a feeling of Christmas.* She released the parking brake and they drove out of the lot. "So," she said, adjusting her dark glasses, "where do you want to go?" She scowled and tightened her lips like she was thinking real hard. "I know!" she said, almost letting go of the wheel. "Sheila Awai, you're a genius!" She turned to Isaac. Her glasses were so dark, he had a hard time seeing the whites of her eyes. "I'm a genius, you know."

Children laughing, people passing, meeting smile after smile. And on every street corner you'll hear . . .

"What's the plan?" Isaac asked.

"Let's go Christmas shopping! Have you finished your Christmas shopping? I haven't."

Silver bells, silver bells. It's Christmas time in the city.

They got on the freeway right by Maryknoll High School and the Shriners Hospital. Sheila shot into the fast lane, pressed a button that sent the car windows up and another that turned on the air conditioner. The vents on the dash were going full blast and the cold air made Isaac's fingers numb. Sheila drove pretty recklessly, switching lanes to avoid slow cars, braking suddenly, not looking in her mirror. And all the while Bing Crosby, the Mormon Tabernacle Choir, Nat King Cole, and Mantovani played Christmas music. "So what did you wind up doing with yourself?" said Sheila, looking at Isaac and smiling. "I mean, after our interview and everything?"

"Well," he said, "there ain't much to tell. I graduated from Farrington High School, went to UH, and wound up being a physical education teacher over at Dole Intermediate School." *Deck the halls with boughs of holly, Fa la la la laaaa* . . . "I'm in my second year of teaching kids how to play soccer and flag football." *Tis the season to be jolly, Fa la la la laaa* . . .

"You mean you didn't follow up your high school career as a brilliant sportswriter?" said Sheila, swerving to avoid hitting a tourist bus.

"I'm afraid not," Isaac said.

"I remember you were quite good," said Sheila. "You had a way of relaxing your subject. It was like you were talking to me, not interviewing me."

"Thanks. Now I spend my days with a lot of nice kids and get paid to run up and down a field in the fresh air."

Isaac couldn't believe the situation. Here he was, being driven around in Sheila Awai's Corvette, telling her his life story. He had never been good at talking about himself, but Sheila seemed to make it so easy. Something about the way she listened. Like she really cared.

"I remember my P.E. teacher," said Sheila. "She was this big, nasty lady. Always swearing at us. I forget her name. Mrs. something. Always blowing her whistle and making us do horrible things like taking laps in the rain. What was her name?"

Sheila got off the freeway and—after a while of running yellow lights and ignoring yield signs—pulled into Ala Moana Center.

"I can't believe it's Christmas already," said Sheila, clapping her hands softly. "Did I tell you I was a close personal friend of Santa Claus?"

"Who?"

Sheila frowned and then smiled. "You must have believed in Santa Claus when you were a little boy." Sheila's eyes brightened, like when the sun catches a piece of glass at a certain angle. "My parents left out cookies and milk for Santa, right under the Christmas tree. When I woke up the next morning, I ran out into the living room, and the cookies and milk were gone. And Santa always left a thank-you note. 'Thank you, Sheila.' I still have those silly letters somewhere."

As Sheila told Isaac these stories about Santa Claus and her childhood, he started thinking about how it was when he was a kid. His grandfather was always telling him about Santa Claus. "Isaac," he would say, "you bettah be good. Or you going wind up with one lump of *kākā* in yoah stocking." For some reason, Isaac could never believe in a fat guy giving presents to all the good little kids in the world. Isaac guessed he was a born cynic, even in kindergarten. What made matters worse was that Isaac sold newspapers on Fort Street Mall, in downtown Honolulu. When Christmas rolled around, all these Santas came out. Like bugs from under a rock. You'd see one ringing a bell here, another one across the street. He knew something was fishy. After all, how many Santa dudes were there? That's what Isaac was thinking as Sheila told him about how much she loved Christmas. But of course, he kept his mouth shut.

"I must have sat on Santa's lap here at Ala Moana Center dozens of times," she said. "We knew each other by first name. 'Hello, Sheila,' he'd say. 'Did you like the tennis racket Santa gave you?' "

O Holy Night, the stars are brightly shining.

Even though the mall was packed with Christmas shoppers, Sheila was able to find a parking space minutes after driving into the lot.

"How'd you do that?" Isaac asked. "It takes me half a day to find a parking space during the holidays."

A thrill of hope, the weary world rejoices, for yonder breaks a new and glorious morn.

Sheila mussed up Isaac's hair with her hand, and the gold

bracelets on her wrist jingled like Christmas bells. "You must bring me good luck."

————————

"WOULD YOU LIKE another beer?"

"Huh? Yes. Yeah. That'd be nice."

Mrs. Kelly, the lady who walked like a hen, took Isaac's empty can. "Puh-*leeese*, Isaac. Call me Lucinda. And help yourself to the spread."

Isaac couldn't believe the food they had here. Back in Kalihi, a big party included beer and maybe a bag of dried cuttlefish. But here, on a huge koa table under a chandelier with a gigantic ice sculpture of either a mermaid or an auto wreck, they had silver plates covered with pineapple, tangerines, broccoli, cheese, ham, snapper, *poke*, sashimi, abalone, scallops, shrimp, lobster, noodles, chicken, duck, pork, and prime rib. Everything looked good, even the things Isaac couldn't identify. The funny thing was that nobody took a lot. People stood around the table, talking about the whiskeys they drank and the people they knew. Two girls nibbled on celery sticks and called someone named Monica a nymphomaniac. Everyone was talking but nobody seemed to want to eat.

Isaac sat down on a soft couch with a plateful of food. He really wasn't very hungry. He felt the way you feel in the waiting room of a dentist's office. His stomach was in knots getting all worked up about Sheila. He had a strong feeling she'd be here soon so he began drawing up a strategy. Maybe when she went to get her food, he'd walk over to her and remind her about the tomatoes at Safeway. "You don't want that one," he'd say. "You want the ones that are firm."

Three guys in matching aloha shirts played Hawaiian music. One guy strummed an acoustic guitar, one guy picked on a slide guitar, and one guy played a stand-up bass. All three sang. It seemed to Isaac that he was the only one paying any attention to them. A pretty girl in beige sat down on the sofa next to him. All she had on her plate was a piece of sushi and some ginger. She picked at the ginger daintily with a pair of chopsticks. "You look like you're doing some daydreaming," she said, smiling and crossing her legs.

"Yeah," Isaac said. "Guess I am."

"What about?"

"What about?" he said, laughing to himself. "I was, uh, just thinking about what would happen if it, uh, if it snowed here in Honolulu. Wouldn't that be something?"

"What?"

"Never mind."

"How long you been here?"

Isaac looked at his watch. "Almost an hour, maybe."

"I wasn't going to come," the girl said. "But I changed my mind when Mrs. Kelly told me some interesting people were supposed to show. Like Denise Santiago. She sings at the Sheraton."

"The one that does those furniture store commercials?"

"Yeah. And even that tennis player. The pretty one—Sheila Awai."

"I've heard the name."

———

ISAAC COULDN'T BELIEVE he was walking through Ala Moana Center with Sheila Awai. He kept hoping David or one of the boys would see him. But wouldn't you know it? Nobody did.

Sheila and Isaac walked randomly—no real destination—stealing glances at each other through full-length mirrors and shop windows as big as buses. Every now and then Sheila stopped and talked to a friend. A radio disc jockey and the fiancé of her doubles partner. A girl she hadn't seen since high school. Several other people asked for autographs. Sheila smiled and asked the people their names, and after she signed her own, told them good-bye and to take care of themselves. Sheila and Isaac walked on, past pots of red-leaved poinsettias, the crowds eating Chinese food from paper plates, the impatient lines in front of the post office, the concrete water fountains filled with koi the color of sparks and fire. They browsed in shops, sprayed perfume on each other, rubbed facial cream samples on their hands, wound the keys of music boxes, sniffed imported teas from India, examined rare and ancient postage stamps through magnifying glasses, compared the prices of stationery and sewing machines and exercise bicycles. And on every loudspeaker, Christmas music. From Handel to the lively "Sleigh Ride" with Christmas bells and temple blocks. *Just hear those sleigh bells jingling, ring-ting-tingling too . . .*

Sheila and Isaac bought rainbow sherbet ice-cream cones and stopped in front of a men's clothing store. In the window, mannequins with nylon hair and gold cufflinks stood at a cocktail party: the men with one hand in their pocket and one hand holding an empty wine glass; the women pointing toward an imaginary horizon. Christmas lights blinked and always, always the sound of the Salvation Army bells echoed above the conversation of the crowds.

"Don't you just love Christmas?" asked Sheila. "I think it's the most exciting time of the year. I remember when I was a little girl, our whole family would be home together for Christmas Eve. It'd be nippy—it gets nippy in Mānoa Valley, Isaac—and I'd wear a jacket and drink cocoa and sit underneath the Christmas tree and smell the fresh pine smell and shake the presents. Dad would finally give up and let me open one gift. 'Just one, Sheila,' he'd say. Of course, I'd take the biggest box. The biggest present that made the most noise when you shook it was always the best." Sheila licked at her ice-cream cone and then licked at her fingers. "And before you knew it, Dad'd let me open another and another . . ."

"I was never much on this Christmas thing."

"Oh, you're so dull, Mr. Kalama."

"Never could relate. Snowmen and skiing and fireplaces. I'll bet there ain't one fireplace in all of Kalihi. In Hawai'i, winter and summer, it's the same smell. And all those pictures of children ice-skating. Hell, the closest I ever got to ice-skating was getting a cardboard box and sliding down the moss in Kalihi Stream."

"I'd bet one of those sports jackets would look great on you." Sheila pointed toward one of the mannequins. "You have nice shoulders."

"Nah. I'm not much into clothes."

"What do you want for Christmas? If you could have anything —anything in the world?"

"Can't think of anything."

"There you go, being boring again. C'mon."

Isaac paused. "I guess I would want everybody to be happy."

"No, no," said Sheila. "Something for real."

———

THE DOORBELL RANG and Isaac looked up. A tall girl with long hair walked in, carrying a bundle of presents. She must have been somebody sort of famous because everybody started whispering and staring. Mrs. Kelly arranged her hair and said welcome, welcome, and how was the flight from L.A.? The girl looked a helluva lot like Sheila. But after a while, Isaac knew it wasn't her. Something about the way she walked, the way she said hello.

The pretty girl in beige sitting on the sofa next to Isaac excused herself and left. He was kind of relieved, in a way. Now he could eat his chicken wings. You can't really enjoy chicken wings if you're self-conscious about using your hands and getting the chicken meat stuck between your teeth. But just as soon as she left, a skinny guy wearing a dress shirt with sleeves rolled up to his elbows and a tie came up to him and smiled. He looked like a lawyer on his lunch break. "There are a lot of pretty girls here," he said.

"Yeah," Isaac answered, looking around the room and seeing

girls in colorful dresses leaning against bookshelves filled with leather-bound art books and encyclopedias. The girls crossed stockinged legs, sipped champagne, waved hands and gold rings, and pointed out on the globe what part of the Mediterranean they had spent their summer vacations in.

"I'm Jet Chong." He extended his hand.

"Isaac Kalama." Jet Chong? *Jet?*

The big guys in matching aloha shirts sang "Mele Kalīkimaka." They did it real well, too. Too bad nobody was listening. *Mele kalī-kimaka is the thing to say on a bright Hawaiian Christmas Day. That's the island greeting that we send to you from the land where palm trees sway . . .*

"Say, uh, Jet. You know, I've been here for a while and I keep hearing a lot of talk about this one girl. Jeez, what's her name? Sandy something. No, that's not it. Darn. Susie, Sarah, Stella, Stephanie . . ."

"Sheila? Sheila Awai?"

"Yeah, that's her. Sheila Awai."

"Oh, yeah. The tennis player. Really nice girl. Real looker, too. She used to give Mrs. Kelly tennis lessons. She's supposed to be stopping by on the way to the airport."

"Airport?"

"Yeah, she's going on this Asian goodwill tournament. Japan, China, Korea, Hong Kong, Taiwan . . ."

"I hope she makes it to the party tonight."

"Oh, she will," said Jet. "She's always late. Say, Eric, have you ever done oyster shooters?"

———

SHEILA AND ISAAC stood in front of the plate-glass window of a music store and looked inside at the rows of drum sets and cymbals, metronomes and music stands, flugel horns and french horns and clarinets and saxophones. He could see their reflection, standing together in the window. He thought they made a great-looking couple.

"Oh, Isaac," said Sheila. "Look at all of the instruments. I play the piano, you know. But I'm not very good. One of my favorites is the Hawaiian version of the 'Twelve Days of Christmas.' The one that goes, 'Faaaaaive beeeeg fat peeeeegs!' " She began to sing softly, to herself. "Four flower lei, tree dry squid, twooo coconut, and one mynah bird in one papaya treeeee."

"I haven't heard that one in years."

"Back in fourth grade our class did a Christmas pageant based on that song. We all had to dress up. My friends Minny and Debra were ten cans of beer and nine pounds of poi. I was tree dried squid."

Behind them a crowd of people had gathered around center stage. Sheila and Isaac walked into the crowd. Isaac figured it was a hula show or a jazz ensemble or some popular comedian doing his nightclub repertoire. But there, next to a Christmas tree with blinking lights, was Santa himself, sitting in a red chair with a kid of about eight or nine on his lap. Parents waved at their children and aimed cameras. A chorus from a preschool sang. The boys had bow ties and the girls wore ribbons in their hair. *Jolly old Saint Nicholas, lean your ear this way. Don't you tell a single soul what I'm going to say. Christmas Eve is coming soon; now, you dear old man.* Sheila had the prettiest look on her face. Her eyes were open wide and her lips moved quietly along with the song. Her cheeks were flushed and for a while, just for a while, Isaac thought a tear might slip past her eyes. "This is so beautiful," she said. "So beautiful."

"Just think," Isaac said. "There might be another Sheila Awai standing in line there somewhere."

Sheila smiled and they walked back to her Corvette.

"Do you want to see my Christmas tree?" said Sheila.

"I'd love to," said Isaac.

From Ala Moana Center they drove to Sheila's house in Mānoa. Up the hill past Punahou School, past Paradise Park. Once, Sheila missed a stop sign and if there had been a car in the intersection, Isaac figured they'd have been dead. When he pointed out what she had done, she said she was sorry. And he couldn't stay mad at her for long because he knew she meant it. Still, he could see the headline in the morning paper: "Sheila Awai and Other in Traffic Collision."

Sheila had a nice place, like many houses in Mānoa Valley. Two story, large garage, sliding doors, rock garden, bonsai plants. Isaac helped carry her shopping bags into the house and told her to keep the tomatoes. She thanked him and told him to make himself at home. Then she turned on the radio. *O little town of Bethlehem, how still we see thee lie.* In one corner of her living room—next to a plate-glass window overlooking Waʻahila Ridge, the Chinese cemetery, and the university—was the largest Christmas tree Isaac had ever seen. Maybe nine, ten feet high. Cardboard angels and peppermint candy canes and felt reindeer and cotton-ball Santa Clauses dangled from the pine-needle branches. The bottom of the tree was surrounded with gifts of all sizes, carefully packaged in elaborate ribbons and wrapping papers. "Ooooh," said Sheila. "Wait till you see the lights!"

She made Isaac close his eyes. Then she hit a switch and giggled and told him to open his eyes. The lights flickered. Gold, blue, red, green. Gold, blue, red, green.

"It's nice," he said, smiling.

"Do you really like it? I hope you don't think I'm just a silly girl. A lot of girls on tour always think I'm just a silly, stupid girl."

"I think you're a sweet girl with a good heart."

Sheila smiled. "I've always had a Christmas tree. Even now, though I live alone and all. It's a nice thing to have around. Like a friend."

It came upon the midnight clear, that glorious song of old. From angels bending near the earth, to touch their harps of gold.

Hanging on her walls were rows of Christmas cards. She caught Isaac looking.

"Lots of friends," he said.

"Not really," said Sheila. "Some of the cards I got when I was six." Many of the cards were yellowed with age. The edges were dog-eared and a few of the cards were water-stained. The glitter had lost its sparkle and the ink was faded and smeared. Many were written in childish hands. To Sheela, luv Laurie. Merrie Christmas, from Jeanne. Season's Grittings, from Jody. *Peace on the earth, good will to men, from heaven's all gracious king.*

"Yeah," said Sheila, smiling and arranging her hair. "It's something nice to read and reread, to remember old friends that have probably forgotten you by now."

The bookshelves in Sheila Awai's living room were filled with old college textbooks—introduction to physics, economics, *Candide*, principles of calculus—and trophies and koa bowls and plaques and ribbons and pictures and magazine covers. The framed pictures and magazine covers all had that loved but neglected look of gifts from very old friends and admirers. There she was, in the *Sporting News*, serving the ball at the Diamond Head Invitational, both arms raised like a musical conductor exhorting her strings to a crescendo; on the cover of *MidWeek* magazine, hugging her racket like a girl hugs a puppy, her head tilted to one side; posing for a photo on the set of *Hawaii Five-0* with Jack Lord, holding a bouquet of roses, during the episode where she played the child tennis star kidnapped by sailors from Singapore; in the last match in the high school state finals against a girl from Lahainaluna, teeth biting lower lip, both arms tense in a backhand, hair blowing in the breeze; shaking the hand of second-seeded Gail Mathias after beating her 6–3, 6–0 in the ILH championships; with the Punahou varsity tennis team, second row, fourth from left, squinting in the sun.

"It's your turn," Isaac said, turning toward her. "I told you my life story. How things have gone since our interview way back when. Now you tell me yours."

She smiled and broke off one of the pine needles of her

Christmas tree and sniffed it. "But there's so much else going on," she protested. "It's Christmas!"

Isaac sat on the couch. *The first noel the angels did say, Was to certain poor shepherds in fields as they lay.*

"Oh, all right," said Sheila, waving the branch like a fairy waving her wand. "But I warn you. It's pretty boring stuff. Let's see. I've played tennis all my life. Tennis, tennis, tennis. Every day my daddy took me outside and we hit balls against the side of the garage. I can still hear the noise. *Pok. Pok. Pok.* I was playing in tournaments at what, nine years old? Went undefeated all the way through college. Got into the mainland tennis circuits and did the tour."

"You must really love tennis," said Isaac.

"Tennis?" Sheila said, smiling and nibbling at her fingernails. "I hate it."

"What do you mean?"

"After a while," she said with a sigh, "you learn that for a person like me, the secret to being happy is not to do what I want to do, but to learn to like the things I have to do."

"That's sad."

Noel, noel, noel, noel. Born is the King of Israel.

"I always have to be somewhere. Practice twice a day, a benefit, a speech, a cocktail party. Oh, Isaac. Just look at my schedule for tomorrow. Practice, tape a commercial, then a luncheon with the governor, then practice, an interview, then a radio spot. I leave for Paris next Tuesday . . ."

"You know, Sheila," Isaac said, "I bet I know something you'd enjoy."

"What?" Her eyes sparkled. "What? Tell me! Tell me!" She was like a little girl.

"Well, I remember when I was younger there used to be a parade, right in Kalihi. There was a marching band, and all the children lined the streets waiting to catch a glimpse of Santa and the candies he threw. The band played the same song over and over, about the guy coming to town."

"*You better watch out, you better not cry,*" Sheila sang. "*You better not pout, I'm telling you why . . .*"

"There we go. That's the one."

"Sounds fantastic. Maybe you can show it to me sometime."

"Maybe one of these days you'll let me."

Sheila sighed. "I have this dream, Isaac, this very silly dream, that one day, one day I'll learn to be the most forgetful girl in the world."

Isaac laughed and Sheila laughed, too. The lights on her tree blinked slowly in the chocolate brown of her eyes. Gold, blue, red, green.

And so I'm offering this simple phrase, to kids from one to ninety-two. Although it's been said, many times, many ways, Merry Christmas to you . . .

———

WHILE LOOKING FOR the bathroom in Mrs. Kelly's house, Isaac wandered into the kitchen by mistake. You know how in most kitchens you see a loaf of bread, or some leftovers wrapped up in plastic, or some breakfast cereal? Here, the only thing Isaac saw was a plant. A fern. But no food, no pans in the sink, no nothing.

In the living room, the three guys in matching aloha shirts were singing "Jingle Bells" in Hawaiian. *Kani kani pele, Kani kani pele, Kani ma'o ma'a nei*

All of a sudden Isaac thought about all of the boys at David's house playing five-card stud and drinking imported beer in green bottles. He didn't know why, but he was sort of envying them. He bet they were having a helluva time. Then a crazy thing happened. He imagined seeing them here—in this room full of Swiss watches and imported prints. Butch's big feet on the koa table, toes tapping to Olomana on the radio. David's cats running around, sharpening their claws on the grand piano. Jessie and Sammy sitting cross-legged on the floor, plucking the metal strings of their guitars. Richie standing by the watercolors talking about some girl he met at the bowling alley. And Darrel "da Barrel" Perry, who once drank three cases of beer in one sitting, belching and passing out on Mrs. Kelly's king-sized bed.

O Christmas tree, O Christmas tree, thy leaves are so unchanging.
The phone rang. Mrs. Kelly picked it up and clapped her hands to get everyone's attention. She said something like listen, listen, Sheila Awai will be here in a half hour. People started talking, real excited, and Jet Chong said something about asking her for backhand pointers. Isaac looked at his watch. Ten to midnight. He had been sitting on the sofa in this Hawai'i Kai art museum, sipping beer and picking at chicken wings, for three-and-a-half hours. He finished his drink, thanked Mrs. Kelly, and walked slowly to the door. The party was pretty much over before it began.

Da Papah Fooball Champion

COUSIN, DIS IS your lucky day. I going introduce you to da All-Time Papah Fooball Champion. You heard of papah fooball, ah? You must've played in elementary school. You get one piece foldah papah. You cut one strip and fold da buggah till da ting is shaped like one small kine, inch-long triangle. Den you and your, what you call, opponent sit about tree, four feet away from each othah, facing each othah. In front of you is da fooball field. You can use one sidewalk or one table or anyting you like. You mark da touchdowns and da fifty-yard line with chalk or masking tape. Den you jus' flick dat papah fooball with your fingers. You and your opponent, back and forth, back and forth. If you flick da ting on your opponent's touchdown, das six points. If you land 'em on da fifty-yard line, you can try for one field goal. Your opponent hold his fingers up like one goalpost and you gotta flick da papah fooball through.

There you have it, papah fooball. Cuz, I was da baddest. Nobody could beat me. One time in intermediate school, during lunch recess, I beat six guys, all in a row. Roscoe, Clint, Roger, Cal, two other clowns. We played in da cafeteria. Dat was da best. Da caf had dose white, slick tables. One good playing field. I even made my own special papah fooball. I covered da ting with masking tape and on one side, I wrote my name with ballpoint pen—Luke—and on da othah side, I drew one red "W," just like da kine get on da side of da Wai-ʻanae Seariders fooball helmet. Choice, ah? My prized possession. Anyway, I was da king. I was wondering if dey had such a ting as, da kine, Professional Papah Fooball.

I went home dat day and, of all people, my kid brother, Kyle, like challenge me.

"Luke," he says, "us go play papah fooball."

So I take out my special papah fooball and we play on da kitchen table. I even let him kick off. Come to find out, he no can play for beans. I start smoking him. *Flick.* Touchdown. *Flick.* Ho, extra point. *Flick.* Anothah touchdown.

"Kyle," I said, "you suck."

"I no like play," he said. "You cheat."

"I cheat?" I said. *Flick.* "Ho, anothah touchdown! How I cheat?"

"You cheat," said Kyle. "I no like play."

"You fricken crybaby," I said. "I should slap your head!"

"I no like play . . ."

"Shaddup." *Flick.* "Ho, brah. Field goal."

Kyle, tears in his eyes, obediently makes da field goalposts with his two hands. I line up my papah fooball and I fly ʻem real good and da buggah go right through Kyle's stoopid fingers and nail ʻem right on his face.

"I quit!" he said.

"Panty," I said. "You like me kick your ass?"

"Boy!" said Dad, walking into da room. "No talk to your bruddah li'dat!"

"We was jus' playing, Dad." What timing.

"Jus' playing, yer ass!" he said. "I hear you talk li'dat to your bruddah again, Luke, and I going kick your sorry ass to Mākaha surfing beach."

Dad looked at me hard and when I looked away, he walked out

of da room. Kyle, da panty bastard, had one smile on his face like he could eat one banana sideways.

————

DAS MY DAD. Me and him, we nevah got along too good. He was always cutting me down. Making me feel like I was one nobody, like him. Dad was one electrician or someting. Fixing telephone poles or whatevah da hell he did. He hated his job. Always came home from work salty. Da only thrills he got out of life was when his buddies came ovah to da house on Saturday nights and played poker. Dey would sit in da living room and drink Crown Royal and V.O. and take each othah's money and tell da same tired stories ovah and ovah again. About da time Harry wen' spear da hundred pound *ulua* diving off Yoks. Da time Leroy was on *Magnum P.I.* Da time Uncle Lloyd had to take off his clothes to avoid da Night Marchers.

One time, was late at night, dey started talking about da war. I guess dey all fought in some war togethah. Dis was kinda long time ago. I was one small kid, and dey must've thought I was sleeping but I wasn't. I couldn't believe da stuffs I was hearing. About running through fields while people was shooting at you. Hearing bullets whistle past your ear. Putting one gun against da enemy guy's head and pulling da triggah. Jeez.

Lemme tell you about my Dad. One time, I was doing my math class homework. Story problems. I hated story problems. Anyway, I was stuck on one, so I started messing around playing papah fooball by myself. Just flicking da ting around, no big deal. My old man came walking in da room—I guess he just came home from work cause his clothes was all dirty—and he tell me, "Luke, what da hell you doing?"

"Homework," I said.

I thought he would just go away, but he nevah.

"No look like you doing your homework," he said. "Look like you fooling around."

"I ain't fooling around," I said.

"Luke," he said, "put dat papah fooball crap away before I slap your head."

"Yeah, yeah."

"Not 'yeah, yeah,' " he said. "I like you study hard, get good grades. Dat way you can go college. Make one living for yourself without having to get your hands dirty every day." He held up his hands, all black with grease. "No be like me."

"Whatevahs," I said, yawning.

"You like lickens, or what?" he said. I no say nothing and he moves closer. "You heard me? You like lickens?"

I figgah I twelve years old and if my old man like beef, I beef 'em. I take him. If he throw, I throw. But before I can do anyting, he walk up to me and false-crack my head so hard—I swear my eyes stay open, but all I see is black. But I no go down, da bastard. I no go down.

———

In high school, I got da chance to play real fooball. Wide receivah. Wai'anae Seariders. Sophomore and junior year, I was pretty much on da bench. But senior year, everybody wen' grad so I was starting. Was pretty cool. Cutting in da lunch line in front all da band geeks. Cruising with da cute chicks.

But you know what? I still played papah fooball. I beat all da guys on da team. My toughest game was against da quarterback. Luthor. Da guy was one good athlete and all. We played aftah practice one day. It took awhile but I convinced him to use my special papah fooball, da one I made with my name and da red "W" and everyting. Cuz, I thought I was going down. Da buggah was good. He was scoring on me left and right. Even with my own fricken fooball. We was playing to thirty. When da score was 24–24, ho, my fingers started for get all tight. I flick my papah fooball and da ting go two inches. Was pretty intense. Luthor tried one field goal but he missed, and I blasted da fooball desperate kine and—*yes!*—da buggah landed on Luthor's touchdown. I won! Luthor, he was cool. He called me one bastard but we went shake hands and drink beer togethah dat night.

Dat week, we was playing da Farrington Governors. Dis was for real kine fooball. Da winnah of da game was going Prep Bowl. Ho, we was tied 12–12 in da fourth quarter. I was doing okay. I had tree catches. Anyway, was late in da game and we had da ball, and da coaches called one play where da quarterback fake one handoff to da running back and throw da ball to me coming across da middle. I remembah we came out of da huddle and Luthor called da play, and I wen' run out and make my cut and I seen da ball coming, right where was supposed to be, and I caught da ting and I was running for da touchdown.

All of a sudden, *poom,* somebody wen' blast me right in da head. Da fooball came out of my hands and da Farrington guy recovered and ran 'em in for one fricken touchdown. I wanted for die. I took off my helmet and walked to da sidelines and nobody wen' look at me, not even Bruddah Luthor, so I just walked to da watercooler and picked up one cup of water even though I wasn't thirsty. Den da receivahs coach, Coach Eli, he walked up to me and let me have it.

"Luke!" he said, his nose touching mine. "What da hell you doing? You let da team down!"

Man, he swore up a storm. Sure enough, we lost da game. Dat was da worst day of my life. I went home and nobody said nothing. Mom, Dad, Kyle. Dey was all still wearing da red-and-black Wai'anae shirts.

I went in my room and lie down on da bed and thought about going into Dad's workshop—where he kept his tools and car parts and fishing gear and free weights—and take out his 30–30, da one he use for hunt, and blow my useless brains out. Das wen Dad came into da room. Oh, great. He like rip into me.

"Luke," he said, "us go outside."

"I no like," I said.

But I went, eventually, just to shut him up. We walked to his workshop and he worked da combination lock and opened da door. I thought he was going hand me his gun and lemme shoot myself. Or maybe he was gonna do it for me. Anyway, we walked inside and he flicked on one light. There, in da middle of da shop, was one koa table.

"Howzit look?" he said. "Made 'em myself."

I was tinking, dis was typical Dad. I lose da biggest fricken fooball game of my life and he drag me out of da house to show me some stupid table he had made.

"It ain't jus' one regulah table," said Dad. "Look closah."

So I looked closah and had all dese markings on top. First, I thought was jus' cheap sale wood. Den I realized, eh, Dad was right. Dis wasn't no regulah table. Dis was one papah fooball field! With touchdowns and fifty-yard line markings and everyting!

"Das for you," he said, putting his arm on my shoulder for da first time in my life. I looked at him, and he was looking at me, and I had to look away because, I don't know why, my eye was getting all funny kine irritated. "Us go try 'em out."

Dad sat on one side of da table and I sat on da othah side. Den I took out my special papah fooball from my pocket and let Dad kick off. Da buggah surprised me. He was one damn good papah fooball playah. I no remembah how long we played, but we played until da cocks was crowing and da sun was shining. And we talked about all kine stuffs dat night. Not just fooball, papah kine and real kine. Jeez, we talked about everyting. And you like know someting? I know you ain't going believe dis, but I swear I no even remembah who won dat papah fooball game. I nevah even care. Honest kine. I tink so was one draw."

———

DA NEXT DAY, last Tuesday, I was in my auto mech class taking apart one Honda Accord. Mr. Ogata, da teachah, said I had to go to da principal's office. I was tinking, jeez, you lose one fooball game, you gotta say sorry to da principal. Whatevahs. Anyway, I walked ovah to da principal's office and he said to call my mom, which I did. "Your faddah died," she said, ovah da phone. She put one funny kine emphasis on da word "died." "He got shock fixing one electric line in Kunia."

We buried Dad dis morning. At da graveyard, dey had one American flag covering his coffin. Like he was one president or someting. During da ceremony, some serious-looking army guys with white gloves walked up to Dad's coffin and slowly took off da American flag. I watched dem fold da flag in half, da long way, and den dey folded 'em into one triangle. Das when da funny ting happened. I realized, eh, dat was exactly how you fold one fricken papah fooball. Den one of da serious-looking army guys handed da triangle-shaped flag to Mom, who placed it on her knees.

Aftah a while, dey started lowering Dad into da ground. People dropped flowers on da coffin. Me, I walked up there and sly kine, I reached into my pocket, took out my special papah fooball—da one with my name and da red "W"—and I dropped da ting into dat deep, dark hole. Dat way, I figgah, Dad can challenge da boys in heaven to papah fooball whenevahs he like get one game going.

When we got home, Mom put Dad's American flag in her bedroom closet. She said tings are gonna be harder now. She was already working two jobs, as one waitress and one maid at some Waikīkī hotel. She says at night, maybe she can drive around and sell flowers in restaurants and bars. Me, I going try score one job at da grocery store down da street. Bag boy. I tink so if I study hard, I still might be able for get decent grades and maybe even go college, like Dad wanted. We'll be okay.

Anyway, there you have it. My old man. Hands down, da All-Time Papah Fooball Champion.

Uncle Martin's Mayonnaise Jar

MY UNCLE MARTIN was a hard-drinking old man who worked as a custodian at Kalihi Elementary School during the day and shaped fiberglass fishing poles in the backyard at night. He was what you'd call your everyday senior citizen, I guess. Liver spots on his chest, balding, going to cockfights in Waipahu cane fields, spending a day's salary at some Waiakamilo Korean bar. The works.

For a while Uncle Martin lived downstairs in our Houghtailing Street house, and he taught me many things. We walked to the swimming pool at Farrington High School every day one summer, and he showed me how to swim and dive. See, Uncle Martin had this belief that Hawai'i was going to get swallowed up by a gigantic tsunami and we'd all have to swim for our lives to Tahiti. Scared the crap out of me, so I listened—and I listened good—to his stories about how he could stay underwater for fifteen minutes without breathing and how, back in the Philippines, he was the champion oyster picker of his village. It didn't take me very long to learn how to swim, and before I knew it, Uncle Martin was teaching me to surf on a long wooden board he called a tanker.

Uncle Martin also taught me how to drive. I must've been about eight or nine, still way too early to get one of them, whaddya call, driving permits. Uncle Martin loved his car—a Camaro with mag wheels, tinted windows, and Centerline rims. When he wasn't sweet-talking a lady or checking out the Vegas line in the sports pages, he was polishing his Camaro or cleaning the oil off the big engine with a chamois-skin cloth. The day he taught me how to drive we went over to Sand Island because he figured there was no way in hell I could kill somebody there—or worse yet, smash up his car. We exchanged seats and Uncle Martin said something to himself in Filipino. Then he told me to relax and keep the wheel steady. His breath smelled like warm beer, even though he hadn't drank in days. He was just one of those guys who always smelled like beer, whether they drank or not. I pumped the gas pedal to the floor because I didn't know how hard you had to press the damn thing, and by the time I heard the engine howl, we were racing up the drawbridge and onto the dirt roads. Dust flew everywhere and Uncle Martin— hands on head—screamed, "Dee brake, you pucker! Dee brake!"

Yeah, Uncle Martin was your everyday old man until he started making bets he couldn't keep on boxing matches. A couple hundred on the shifty middleweight from Mexico. Double or nothing and the jade ring his third wife bought him on the black welterweight from Detroit. He won more than he lost and, for a while, he looked like he was in pretty good shape. Fancy clothes, expensive whiskey, gold chains, lots of friends. It was all coming up roses until the night he put five grand on a guy named Avilla—a fighter he never even saw —who was supposed to be a sure-shot because he was a *manong* and a cousin of the cook at Uncle Martin's favorite restaurant, Lita's Filipino Cuisine. Avilla was dropped in the third round with a right to the temple, and all of a sudden, Uncle Martin owed five thou to a guy named Jammer Kalai who had an office over a small packing warehouse in Kaka'ako. Five thousand bucks. That's when Uncle Martin packed his bags and left for Los Angeles.

I was eleven and in the sixth grade when Mom told me I'd

gotten a letter from Uncle Martin. I was pretty excited to hear from him, even though he didn't have enough postage stamps on the letter and Mom had to pay the balance to the mailman. Uncle Martin said he was sick and in the hospital. He said I was his only friend and that he wanted me to visit him in Los Angeles. I didn't have the guts to tell him I didn't have the two hundred bucks it would take to buy myself a ticket to Los Angeles, so I wrote back and told him, yeah, I'd be there.

It was a Saturday and we were all in the living room listening to my older brother, Vaughn, play the electric guitar. The whole family was there, pretty much. Me, Vaughn, my younger brother, Jeremiah, and my two little sisters, Cissy and Elise. Vaughn was into real loud stuff like Led Zeppelin and Deep Purple, and he must've played us that song "Stairway to Heaven" about six million times.

What drove Vaughn crazy was our aunties and how cute they thought he looked when he played his electric guitar. I mean, put yourself in his position. Here he was, trying to be a bad, mean dude. Right out of a rock-and-roll magazine. Smashing guitars to pieces, blowing up amplifiers, swearing at cops, picking up panties that crazed girls tossed on stage. Vaughn was growing his hair long and would have given his right leg and his entire baseball card collection for six hairs to sprout on his ninth-grade chin. He was learning how to smoke cigarettes without inhaling and was always talking about tattooing skulls and crap on his body. But whenever Aunty Lucinda came over with her knitting needles and banana bread, she'd always do the same thing. She'd wipe her feet on the welcome mat, take off her hat, come into the house, and say, "Oh, you so cute, Vaughn. Just like dat boy in da Pahtridge Family."

"Da hell you talking about?" Vaughn would say. "I ain't like dat! I bad! Da meanest! I kick his ass!"

"Where you going, talking to your Aunty Lucinda like dat?"

"Das how all da rock stars talk."

"How da song go?"

"Which song? Da Who? Black Sabbath? AC/DC? Rush? Jimi Hendri—"

"*C'mon world, there's a song dat we singing. C'mon get happy . . . ,*" sang Aunty Lucinda.

After I got the news about Uncle Martin, I was really messed up. I knew I had to see him, but I didn't know where I could pick up two hundred dollars for a plane ticket to Los Angeles. I thought about asking my parents for the money but I knew they wouldn't give it to me. See, they never seemed to care much for Uncle Martin. When his fifth wife found him fooling around with another lady, she kicked him out of their 'Aiea house. Dad said he could stay with us for a couple of days. After the first year, I could tell the family was getting real tired of having Uncle Martin around. When he walked into the living room, everyone stood up and left. Vaughn always complained about Uncle Martin leaving his hairs all over the bathtub. Dad complained about putting a case of beer in the fridge and coming home from a hard day's work and finding only four left. Mom complained that whenever Uncle Martin made *dinuguan,* he left pig blood in the kitchen sink.

I walked over to the bowling alley and played some pinball. I always played pinball when I had something on my mind. I didn't have any quarters with me, but I did have a screwdriver that I used to fool around with the machines to get me as many free games as I wanted. It's sorta like screwing with a pay phone to scab off a free call. But somehow you learn that for some stupid reason, pinball ain't too much fun unless you're putting in your own quarters. So, after a while, I put the screwdriver away and went into the bathroom to take a leak. A guy everyone called Damaged Bob sat on a toilet brushing his teeth. He was supposed to know everything. Damaged Bob wore an old blue sweater, and he had gray hair that fell past his shoulders. When I walked into the bathroom I smiled at him and he gave me a grunt. At least he'd noticed me.

" 'Scuse me, brah." I said. "I get one problem and folks say you know everyting." Damaged Bob was brushing his teeth without toothpaste. He was using something that looked more like milk. Boy, did he smell. Like the elephant cage at the zoo after it rains. "Anyway, I get one friend who sick and he like see me. Problem is, he stay in Los Angeles and I no more da money to get up there."

Damaged Bob looked at me for a long time. It was very quiet and I could hear somebody flushing the toilet on the other side of the wall in the ladies' bathroom. "You da guy who went eat my mortgage," he said as he walked past me and out the bathroom. "You one terrible landlord."

I ALWAYS PROMISED myself that when I grew up, I'd have a son who played quarterback for the University of Hawai'i Rainbows and won the Heisman trophy, and I'd have a daughter who worked in a flower shop. Her name was gonna be Cheryl. See, there was this girl named Cheryl Nitta who baby-sat for a couple of kids in the neighborhood. She was a Japanese girl, I guess, but she really didn't look all that Japanese. She looked more like a mixture of all sorts of stuffs. Anyway, she was about fourteen or so and worked in a Nu'uanu flower shop and baby-sat for some of the neighborhood kids.

She was the talk of the neighborhood, especially with my brother Vaughn. He always had some cornball excuse to pass the Fitsimmons' house—that was the name of the couple Cheryl baby-sat for, Fitsimmons—and he was always spouting off about how she loved him and what they did in the bushes and how she once asked him if he'd like to get married.

After I left the bowling alley and got Damaged Bob's smell out of my clothes and hair, I walked to the Fitsimmons' house to see if Cheryl was around. She was probably the smartest person I knew, and I figured if anybody could help me with my problems, it was her. Cheryl was sitting under a lychee tree, and the two brats were digging their noses and running around half-naked. Cheryl smiled when she saw me. She wore a pink hibiscus in her hair and a pink dress with white stripes. She was doing a composition for her English class, she said, and I sat down and watched her write. She wrote her letters real slow and round. Now that I think about it, it seems like every time I saw her, she was writing something.

"Have you evah gone anywhere real far, far away?" I said.

"My parents took my sister and me to Boston once," Cheryl said, looking puzzled. "Why?"

"I going see my Uncle Martin in Los Angeles."

"Los Angeles? Are you going with your family? Or just Vaughn? Or—"

"I going by myself."

"Los Angeles is a big place."

"I been to big places. One time, I caught da bus from here all da way to Ala Moana Shopping Center, by myself."

"Wow!" said Cheryl, smiling.

"What dis?" I asked, pointing to a lavender-colored paperback she had in her three-ring binder.

"Oh, this?" she said, holding up the book. "It's nothing." It was one of those romance novels girls buy in supermarkets. Her cheeks turned real red and pretty, and I figured maybe eleven-year-olds like me weren't too young to fall in love or whatever you call it. "You must be close to your uncle," she said.

"He taught me lots of tings. And he was always buying stuffs for people, flowers or wine or televisions . . ."

"He sounds like a nice man. He must have had lots of friends."

"No. I was his only one. He said so."

"And since you're his only friend, you have to go see him."

"Yup."

"Los Angeles is far away. And it costs a lot of money to get there."

"Two hundred dollars."

"Where are you going to get two hundred dollars?"

"I don't know. All I know is Uncle Martin sick."

Cheryl took the hibiscus out of her hair and placed it in my hand. "You're a real gentleman." I smiled. I couldn't wait to tell Vaughn. "I tell you what," she said. She opened her purse and took out a five-dollar bill. "I was gonna buy myself a super gigantic sundae. But you take this, to kinda get you on your way. It's just a small gift."

I thanked her and folded up the five-dollar bill real slow and neat. I smiled and it was funny because I had to look away because something had caught in my eye—dust or something—and it was poking at my eyeball and my vision was getting all blurred, but it was the best feeling in the world.

WE LIVED IN a raised house, and to get underneath, you had to crawl through a small door with an old copper-colored combination lock. I opened the lock on my first try. The air smelled like dirt, dust, and spider webs, and it made me sneeze. Above me, I heard footsteps and voices and pipes running. Vaughn followed me in. He wore Dad's Old Spice. Vaughn tried switching on an overhead bulb but when he tugged at the chain it fell to the ground. The rusty chain looked like a centipede in the dirt.

"I don't know what all dis fuss about Uncle Martin is about," said Vaughn. "Da buggah was da weirdest, dirtiest, crookedest bastard in Kalihi. In da world. He probably not even in da hospital, not even sick. If you going work dis hard for get two hundred dollars, you should spend da money on someting important. Like one new stereo or—"

"Uncle Martin wasn't weird," I said.

"Oh yeah?" said Vaughn. "What about da time Tanksgiving?"

When he got drunk on da Cutty Sark and he went into da rubbish can and collected all da turkey bones and pasted dem togethah with glue?"

I gathered some old jigsaw puzzles, a box filled with board games like checkers and Monopoly, two boxes of comic books and magazines, and piled them all on an old red wagon and wheeled them out.

"You know what else we should do?" asked Vaughn. "Go fishing. Like in da old days. Catch maybe fifteen, twenty fish and sell 'em. Remembah how we used to do it? Some *papio*, some *uhu*. Big money. We can make your two hundred dollars in one aftahnoon. Figgah we gotta bring at least tree ice chests."

We got our rods and reels, borrowed Dad's tackle box, hosed down three dirty ice chests, and drove to Hale'iwa. Vaughn had one of those stick things in the truck that made everything smell good and it was a pleasant drive. We went the long way, going through the Wilson Tunnel and cruising past Kualoa and Swanzy and Kahuku. When we got to Hale'iwa, we unloaded the three coolers and sat on the beach. *'Ahi* was going for about ten bucks a pound and if we caught several of those babies, I figured we'd be on easy street. "I hope da ice chests big enough for all da fish I catch," said Vaughn, placing a piece of shrimp on his hook. "I feel lucky today."

"Uncle Martin nevah used shrimp for bait," I said. "He always used lure."

"Das because Uncle Martin nevah had da money for buy fresh bait. He was always spending his bucks on booze or some wahine or some bum fighter."

"Too bad Uncle Martin no stay here. He used to tell me when he was youngah in da Philippines he used to go for da tuna, da *aku*, with one hand-line. And, eh, he caught one marlin, you know. Off Moloka'i. Twelve hundred pounds. Fought da buggah for two weeks. He evah told you dat story?"

"A hundred times."

We sat on the beach until the sun moved clear across the sky and turned everything pink and orange, like fire. We wound up with six *wekes*, maybe four inches long. We tied them up in the plastic bag we brought the shrimp in and threw the three coolers' worth of ice into the ocean. No one said a word. Six four-inch *wekes*. I wanted to bury those pitiful bastards in the sand and forget about them as quick as possible.

"Maybe we should sell da reels," said Vaughn.

The next day we played touch football against these guys from 'Ālewa Heights. Vaughn was our quarterback. He was the only one who could throw a tight spiral and toss the bomb over telephone wires. He was also the oldest. I was the receiver.

"Run to da laundry pole," said Vaughn in the huddle, his right index finger scratching patterns on the open palm of his left hand. "Fake left, den cut to da fence." We clapped and lined up. My younger brother, Jeremiah, sat on the front steps of our house, wiping an old jar with a piece of chamois skin Uncle Martin used to polish his Camaro. Vaughn did a little dance. "Dis next play is dedicated to my future wife, Cheryl Nitta!" Jeremiah looked up from the jar and cheered.

"Cut it out, Vaughn!" I said.

"Hut!" he said. I centered the ball and ran to the laundry pole and Vaughn threw the ball at me. I turned and saw it coming—a tight, quick bullet—but it bounced off my hand and landed on the green onion plants of the Chinese man on the other side of the fence.

"*Stoo*-ped!" said Vaughn, disgusted.

I was about to climb over the wire fence and get the ball when the old man came out of his garage and beat me to it. He stooped slowly and examined the football like he'd never seen one in his life, which he probably hadn't. It was only an old Nerf held together with black electrician's tape, but Vaughn ate with it and slept with it. The old man had glasses resting on top of his head and carried a paintbrush. He wasn't smiling. The ball had bent some of his green onion stalks, and he shook his head slowly as he examined the damaged plants. Then he picked up the ball and, without returning it, walked back to his garage. Vaughn swore—I don't know if it was at the old man or me—and stuck out his middle finger. Then he turned to Jeremiah. "What you carrying around one empty pickle jar for?"

"Dis ain't one pickle jar," said Jeremiah. "Dis one mayonnaise jar. I going put all da money we collect in here so Jesse can go see Uncle Martin."

"Das a good idea," I said, smiling.

"I know," said Jeremiah.

"Das one stoo-ped idea," said Vaughn. "You ain't going be able for collect one dollar in dat jar."

I took out Cheryl's five-dollar bill and handed it to Jeremiah.

"Wow!" said Jeremiah, his eyes wide open.

"Where da hell you got dat kind money from?" said Vaughn.

I smiled. Cissy and Elise came up the driveway. Elise was the younger one—she was five—and she dragged the red wagon I'd found underneath the house. Taped to the wagon was a cardboard sign that read, Fresh Fish, Ten Dollars. Cissy was seven and she had pink ribbons in her hair. She carried her coin purse and wore her best dress, the one Mom had bought at the Liberty House Zooper Sale. Cissy had one of those coin purses made out of pink vinyl that all the girls her age seemed to have, with pictures of princesses in long dresses with flowers in their hair, playing with chipmunks and raccoons. When I asked her what she was carrying the purse for, she said it was for change. I looked in her purse and there was a paper clip, some colorful sheets of origami paper, four nickels, and a quarter. Cissy and Elise had wrapped each fish neatly in a Ziploc bag full of ice cubes. The wet plastic bags made pools of water in the wagon, and the dirt that had been caked in the corners for years colored the water a dark brown, like the bottom of a cup of hot chocolate.

"And what you all dressed up for?" asked Vaughn. "Where you going?"

"We going sell dese fish," said Cissy.

"Yeah," said Elise. She always agreed with whatever Cissy said.

Vaughn looked at the cardboard sign taped to the wagon. "I no tink people going pay ten bucks for six four-inch-long *wekes*."

"Not ten dollars for six," said Cissy. "You no can read, or what?"

"Yeah," said Elise. "No can read, or what?"

"What?" said Vaughn. "Da sign says, Fresh Fish, Ten Dollars."

"Ten dollars *each*," said Cissy.

"Ten dollars each?" repeated Vaughn. "Ten dollars each? What dat? Tree dollars a inch?"

Cissy closed her eyes haughtily, like she saw people do on TV, and told Elise to push the wagon. The wheels on the asphalt made a loud rattling sound, and the water from the melted ice cubes in the Ziploc bags spilled out of a rusted hole in the corner of the wagon and made a dark trail down the driveway.

———

IT WAS ONE of those old stores on Hotel Street, right where all the buses pass, that bought electric fans, old glassware, broken watches, and rings from couples who no longer loved each other. Vaughn and me filled several cardboard boxes full of our old comic books and a bunch of junk we found underneath the house. Mom had a pile of records she wanted to get rid of—Elvis in Hawaiʻi, the Carpenters, Broadway soundtracks like *My Fair Lady* and *The King and I*, Perry Como, Johnny Mathis, Frank Sinatra, and Mantovani.

"I don't know why I doing dis," said Vaughn. "I should be checking out my honey, Cheryl."

"She ain't your honey," I said.

"Oh yeah?" said Vaughn. "Das what you tink. You should have seen what we did in da bushes last time."

The owner of the store was a young guy with wire-rimmed glasses and long brown hair. His forearms were very thin and his fingernails were thick and dirty. His store was dark because it had no windows. The room smelled of dust and urine and cigarette ash and automobile exhaust from the street. There was a ceiling fan on the roof that needed oiling, and it made a *put-put* sound as it rotated slowly above us. Next door was a bar and I could hear the music and the clack of billiard balls through the thin plaster walls. When we walked in, the man was behind his cash register reading a *Playboy* magazine but he wasn't checking out the pictures, and Vaughn looked at him funny.

We dropped the boxes on the desk in front of the man and he looked through them very carefully, holding the comic magazines to the light and checking the spines, I guess, for creases. I could tell by the way he was looking we were gonna get some money from him. The guy was like a bad poker player with a king-high straight, his eyes lighting up like a jackpot machine. A noise came from behind one of the wooden shelves, like a rat's body glancing against a wall. *Fffttt.* Just like that. I began to count in my head. A hundred comics at—say, a quarter or so a piece—would be, uh, would be . . .

Vaughn walked around the store with his hands in his pockets and I caught up with him. The walls were covered with all sorts of posters from movies I'd never heard of. Except *Dracula*. I'd seen that one on the late show. Superman comic books in tight-fitting plastic bags hung in neat rows on the wall. Some of them were selling for fifty bucks a shot. I couldn't understand that, because most of them were yellow and looked a hundred years old. I figured if those ancient-looking comic books sold for that much, mine—which were newer—would bring in twice as much. A hundred comic books at fifty dollars a piece and I could walk into Uncle Martin's hospital room with that set of golf clubs he always talked about buying.

There was an old samurai sword on one of the shelves. Vaughn cautiously pulled the sword halfway out of the glossy case and ran his fingers along the stainless-steel blade. It was dull and didn't cut. "Lemme ask you one personal question," said Vaughn, putting the sword back. "Just between you and me. Why da hell you going through all dis headache for Uncle Martin? You got da whole family going crazy. Jeremiah, Cissy, Elise, jeez, even me. For Uncle Martin? I bet you no even remembah what da guy looked like."

"I don't," I said. "But I remembah how he used to teach me how play nose flute and how he nevah forgot to buy me one Christmas present and how he used to say it was bad luck to clean yard if there was a big football game on TV."

"All I remembah about da dude," said Vaughn, "is how he used to give me a twenty-dollar bill on my birthday if he won big at da cockfights, but he always spelled my name wrong on da damn card. Vaughn. V-O-N."

"He taught me how cut one deck of cards five, six, seven times and always come up with da ace of spades on top. And I remembah how he used to teach me how for shadow box. Right on da garage wall."

"All I remembah is how every Friday night, he used to bring some lady into his room and he'd lock da door and da walls would be banging and shaking."

"Remembah da time Uncle Martin made us tie him up with rope?" I said. "And den he told us close our eyes, and thirty seconds later when we went open 'em, only had da rope?"

Vaughn leaned on the glass case and pointed at a turquoise pendant on a gold chain. "Can you imagine dat around Cheryl's neck?" Vaughn said. Then he whistled. "I wish I had da cash to buy dat for her."

I looked at the price. "Maybe I'll buy it."

"You?" The way Vaughn looked at me, he didn't have to say anymore.

We walked back to the man behind the counter, who wrote something on a piece of paper. Vaughn fingered through his *Playboy* magazine. The man gave the paper to Vaughn. I looked over Vaughn's shoulder. The paper read, "Three dollars. Cash." Three dollars for a hundred comic books, a box of records, and a handful of toys, games, and assorted junk. The man started whistling between his teeth. Vaughn looked at me and I shrugged, and then Vaughn looked at the man behind the counter and nodded his head. The man opened the cash register with a key attached to a piece of string and gave Vaughn three of the ugliest looking dollar bills I had ever seen. One had been nearly ripped in two and repaired with a piece of yellowing Scotch tape. The others had reddish stains, like spray paint. It looked like the kind of money I imagined cops took out of the pockets of dead people found floating facedown in Nuʻuanu Stream.

"Why no at least throw in da magazine?" said Vaughn.

The man with the glasses looked at the girl on the cover for a minute. "Take 'em," he said.

"*Mahalo*," said Vaughn, and he rolled the magazine and placed it in his back pocket.

THE POOL HALL smelled like molasses.

That's about the only way I can explain it. Sorta like when you drove through Waipahu, by the old sugar mill. That was the smell. It would take a sap like Vaughn to want to walk through a Hotel Street pool hall. "One game," he said. "Just one game."

There were two long wooden benches in the pool hall, one near the door and one in the back, against the wall. Old Filipino men in white undershirts sat on the benches reading the morning paper and speaking Tagalog or Ilocano. They smoked cigars and gestured with their hands and slapped their knees when they laughed. Vaughn picked up a cue stick from a rack on the wall. I could feel the Filipino men watching us.

"Let's get out of here," I said.

"Nah," said Vaughn. "Stoo-ped."

A man with a gauze bandage on his right eye walked over to us. A girl with a short black leather skirt and red hair and too much eye makeup followed. She was chewing gum and cracking it loudly. The man wore a polyester blue aloha shirt two sizes too large and gray pants that dragged on the floor. He looked at Vaughn but didn't smile. He came so close to us I could see a yellow spot of pus in the middle of the gauze bandage on his eye. He smelled like an old cigar.

"So," he said. "Like play?"

"Shoots," said Vaughn.

"Stripes and solids?" The man looked at Vaughn and smiled. "Keep it simple."

"How 'bout a side bet?" said Vaughn.

I tugged at his shirt. "What da hell you tink you doing?"

Vaughn smiled. "What da hell you worried about?" he said, whispering out of the corner of his mouth. "You lucky, brah. I doing you one favor. Besides, da buggah only get one eye."

"Five bucks?" the guy said.

"Ten," said Vaughn.

"Cocky bastard, ah?" said the man. "Das good. Ten."

Vaughn turned to me and winked. "Like taking candy from a one-eyed baby."

"Chalk my stick, Fifi," the man said to the girl in the short skirt.

"He get one chick for chalk his stick," I told Vaughn.

"Fifi," said Vaughn. "Das French, ah?"

"She do anyting you want," said the man.

Vaughn broke and that was the last time he stood in front of the table. In less than five minutes, the guy dropped every solid-colored ball. The girl stood behind him, clapping softly every time he sank a shot. I looked at Vaughn. When the one-eyed dude sank the eight ball, I swear Vaughn's face turned greener than a traffic light. He reached into his pocket and took out a ten-dollar bill. The man kissed the bill and put it into his shirt pocket. "Eh," he said, raising a finger, "you like earn your money back?"

"Double or nothing?" asked Vaughn. "Nine ball?"

"Naw," said the man, laughing. "Naw." He stroked his chin and looked at the wooden floor covered with ash and cigarette butts. "See, uh, I one businessman. Busy like hell, running around here and there like one chicken without one head. Sometime, no more time clean yard. Pick up here and there."

"No tanks," I said.

Vaughn pushed me away. "What da hell you talking about?" he said to me. "You like see Uncle Martin or not? Easy money." He turned back to the one-eyed dude. "Just pick up here and there?"

"Das all," the man said, shrugging. "Das all."

"How much?" Vaughn asked.

"I'm a nice guy," the man said. "I give you twenty."

We hopped in the man's Valiant, picked up Dad's lawn mower, and drove to a small house in Pālolo. The place was a mess. Pikake grew wild on the chain-link fence surrounding the property. The grass was at least a foot high, and scattered around the yard were the scrapped body of a car, a stove, a fridge without a door, a TV with a broken screen, and a termite-eaten plywood desk. Someone had written something with yellow chalk on the windshield of the scrapped car.

"Lemme know when you boys *pau*," said the man. Then he went inside the house and Vaughn pushed the lawn mower over the tall weeds.

"Da tings I do for you," Vaughn said, looking at me like I was a dog who'd just messed up the carpet. "I should be at da Fitsimmons' house, talking to Cheryl." I walked over to the icebox. "Leave dat ovah there," said Vaughn. "We take care dat latahs."

"I going move 'em," I said. "Da ting in my way."

"Da buggah too heavy for you, kiddo."

"No call me kiddo. I can do 'em!"

"Do 'em, den!"

I bent and grabbed the corner of the icebox. It was heavier than I thought so I pushed harder. My palm was wet with sweat and it slipped, and I caught my hand on a jagged piece of metal and ripped the back of my forearm open. The blood spilled onto the icebox and I tried to wipe it off so Vaughn wouldn't see, but the more I rubbed it, the more it smeared. It got on my hands and I tried wiping it on the grass. It stained the light-colored grass a dark red.

"Help me move dis damn stove!" said Vaughn, his face flushed and his hair stuck to his forehead. "Hot like hell," he said. "Da tings I do for you." We bent down and worked the stove into a corner of the yard. Vaughn was too busy giving instructions to notice I was bleeding to death.

In two hours we'd moved the heavy appliances to one corner—next to the scrapped car—swept up the broken pieces of rust and the jagged pieces of glass with a dustpan made out of a Wesson Oil can, cut the grass, and trimmed the pikake plant.

"Twenty bucks is twenty bucks," said Vaughn. He had taken off his shirt and wrapped it around his head like a bandanna. My arm felt very heavy, and when I moved it—even slightly—a sharp pain ripped through my gut. I waited below as Vaughn climbed the stairs and knocked at the door. The man with the gauze bandage came out. He had changed his shirt. "Yes suhs," he said. "What can I do for you?" He looked at us as if he didn't know who we were.

"We finish," said Vaughn, holding out his hand.

" 'Scuse me?"

I stood up and the throbbing shot to my head. I looked at my arm. The gash was wide and green. I closed my eyes, but the pain got worse so I opened them again.

"You owe us twenty bucks," said Vaughn.

The man reached into his pocket and took out a brown wallet. He opened the billfold and showed us that it was empty. "Ain't got no twenty bucks, friend. Sorry."

"But we cleaned your damn yard . . ."

"You deaf? Get lost before I kick your ass."

"You fu—"

"Watch your mouth, boy."

The man shook his head and slammed the door. I could feel my pulse banging all the way up to my head from the slice in my forearm. Vaughn took off his shirt and shook his hair, and the perspiration flying in the air made a halo around his head. Then he kicked the chain-link fence and looked at me.

"Eh," he said, "you all right, or what?"

————

THE LAST TIME I had a cut this big was the day I stepped on a nail in my bare feet at the Kapālama Canal, and the nail went through my foot and came out on the other side between my second and third toes. Uncle Martin took real good care of it, though. Problem was, there was an electrical blackout that night so Uncle Martin had to light matches and hold them up to my foot to see. The matches were so close I swear I could feel the fire on my heel. He put some iodine stuff on my foot, then wrapped it tight with a torn diaper. It hurt like hell, but Uncle Martin said it was supposed to hurt like hell because the medicine was cleaning the cut. Then, after all that, he whipped my behind for walking around barefoot in the first place.

We brought Dad's lawn mower home and put it back in the toolshed. Then Vaughn started fixing his hair and straightening the wrinkles in his shirt and suggested we go visit Cheryl at the Fitsimmons' house. He loved his hair, the bastard. He looked at my arm, shook his head, and let out a whistle. "When we get ovah there, lemme do da talking. I tink so her father is one doctor."

Cheryl sat under the lychee tree at the Fitsimmons' house, eating apricots out of a plastic bag and helping the two brats with their Bugs Bunny coloring books. By now, I had to hold my cut arm with my good one to steady it. I felt the beating of my heart in my hand and the weight of my footsteps shooting up through my temple. It was like with every pulse, every footstep, somebody was false-cracking the side of my head.

The way Cheryl looked at me and my arm when we walked into the yard, I must have been in pretty bad shape. She told Vaughn to help himself to the apricots and he winked at me as she ran into the house. "Da girl loves me," he said. She came back with some cotton balls and a small, red bottle of Mercurochrome. She put the Mercurochrome on my cut and it was like sticking needles in my arm. I did everything I could to keep from yelling.

"Is it sore?" Cheryl asked, and when I nodded she started to blow gently on my arm. I got a funny feeling in my stomach, like when you're going down on the Ferris wheel at the carnival. "There. Is that better?"

I nodded.

"Whew, Cheryl," said Vaughn. "Lucky ting your old man is one doctor."

"My father teaches math," she said, looking confused.

"Math?" said Vaughn, slapping his head and laughing nervously. Then he looked at me. "See, Jesse, I told you her father is one teacher. What's dis business you giving me about her father being one doctor?"

Vaughn started talking to Cheryl about playing the electric guitar.

"You play guitar?" said Cheryl, impressed. "Are you like the guy on that TV show? *The Partridge Family*?"

"Well," said Vaughn, "not really."

"I love those guys," said Cheryl. "Do you know a lot of their songs?"

"Uh, to tell you da truth . . ."

"Oooh. Which ones?"

"Oh," said Vaughn, waving a hand. "All of 'em. You name 'em, I play 'em."

VAUGHN GOT A part-time job over at Ace's Grocery Store on Gulick Avenue, past the banks and the fire station. He said he got the job to help me raise money to see Uncle Martin, but I knew him better than that. He worked mostly as a butcher, cutting and weighing meats, but on weekends he sat behind the cash register while the old Japanese lady who owned the store stayed home and took care of the house. She was a widow. Vaughn liked the weekends, when business was slow and he could listen to the Dodgers play baseball on the small clock-radio the old lady had won a long time ago for rolling a two-thirty-four at a Kam Bowl tournament.

One Saturday, after *The Flintstones* and *Scooby Doo,* Jeremiah and me headed over to the store. Jeremiah held Uncle Martin's mayonnaise jar under his arm, the way a running back carries a football. The jar was half full with coins and crumpled up dollar bills rolled into tight balls that resembled tiny cabbages. All the money we had collected for Uncle Martin so far was in the jar. The five dollars Cheryl gave me, the three dollars we got from the man we sold our stuff to. It was all in there.

"Whassup?" said Vaughn as me and Jeremiah walked in. Jeremiah put the mayonnaise jar on the counter next to the cash register. "How's da dough?"

"Good," said Jeremiah. He took out a notebook from his back pocket. "Sixteen dollars, fifty-four cents."

"Whew," said Vaughn. "Can buy one nice football with dat kind money. Leather and all. Lemme see dat jar." Jeremiah moved the mayonnaise jar away from Vaughn. "Eh, seen my honey Cheryl, or what? If you see her, tell her dat I like—"

"I should get one job like dis," I said.

"You too young," said Vaughn.

"I got anothah letter from Uncle Martin today," I said, changing the subject. "Da doctors say he still sick but he say he feel like one million bucks. He like eat steak and shrimp but dey only feed him soup and crackers and Jell-O."

"Da buggah ain't sick," said Vaughn. "He ain't in no hospital."

"He said get one nurse in his ward, longest legs he evah seen."

An old lady walked into the store with an umbrella and a shopping bag and asked what kind of fish was on sale.

"Uh," said Vaughn. "Snapper. Snapper good today."

The lady nodded and followed Vaughn between two shelves of breakfast cereals and Oreo cookies and animal crackers. The whole store had the sweet smell of laundry detergent. Behind the meat counter, Vaughn held up the snapper with two hands, and the lady squinted to get a closer look at the fish, and said, "Gimme da whole ting."

"Scaled?"

"Yes. Thank you."

Vaughn winked and put the fish on the cutting board and ran the scaler from the fish's tail to head, tail to head. Scales flew everywhere like snow. I ain't never seen snow but I imagine that's what it looks like. Scales flying around in Ace's Grocery Store. Vaughn then rinsed the fish and told me to get the broom. He got a large knife and cut a line on the fish's underside from the mouth to the tail and stuck his hand in the gill area and pulled out the red innards. He threw the dark, soft pieces into a milk carton and rinsed the fish and his hands under the faucet. Then he wrapped the snapper in pink paper and wrote the price on it with a red wax pencil.

After the lady left, we sat at the adding machine to see how much money Vaughn would earn in two weeks. The total came out to something like a hundred dollars.

"I going try get one job, too," I said.

"I told you awready," said Vaughn. "You too young."

"If you can, I can."

———————

I WAS WITH Mom at the supermarket buying milk—Vaughn drank about a hundred gallons a week, said it kept his bones strong—when I saw a guy standing around doing not too much of anything. He wore a tie and a big, shiny name tag and his hair was neat and smelled sweet, so I figured he must be a manager or something. I was carrying my slippers in my hand because I liked to walk barefoot on the cool tile floor.

"Are you a manager?" I said.

"Yeah," he said. "Why?" He took out a pencil from behind his ear and began writing on a notepad he had in his back pocket.

"I like your store," I said, messing around for the right words. "I like da way you got da shelves all neat and lined up and organized. Sorta like one library. Must take a lot of work to keep it neat, huh?"

My mother was looking at a humongous watermelon. I loved watermelons but always wound up swallowing the seeds.

"A lot of work," said the manager guy.

"How much money you make?" I said.

"Eleven-fifty an hour. Why?"

"Eleven-fifty? Jeez . . ." That was way more than Vaughn. "You need any help? I could mop up da floor. Chase away all da guys dat hang around da magazine stand all day. Listen. 'Go home. Dis ain't no library.' How's dat? Pretty good, ah?"

"How old are you? Nine?"

"Eleven."

"Listen. You gotta be fifteen to work."

"Fifteen, nothing!" I said. "I can do whatevah anybody here can do!" I pointed to a guy bent on one knee, stamping prices on a bunch of cans. He got up and moved the cardboard box full of cans to another shelf. Then he bent down on one knee and started stamping the cans again.

"I can do dat," I said. "Da guy is a wimp! I can move two of dose boxes. Tree."

"You gotta have a work permit."

"Look, can't you make an exception? I need da money. My Uncle Martin—"

"Uncle Martin or Aunt Harriet or what, you gotta be fifteen."

———

DAD SAT IN front of the tube watching a rerun of *The Wild Wild West* and drinking a can of beer with the electric fan at his back. He wore a white undershirt and boxer shorts that almost went down to his knees. "What dis I hear about you folks trying for earn money?" he asked me. "Vaughn getting one job, Jeremiah walking around with one pickle jar, Cissy and Elise trying for sell dose tiny fishes . . ."

"For Uncle Martin. In Los Angeles."

"Uncle Martin? I should've known. Dat good-fer-nutting-son-of-a-bitch bastard."

"He taught me how pop firecrackers. Remembah? Roman candles and cherry bombs?"

"Urrhhppuurghhgghh," said Dad, letting out a loud belch. "Only one way for make money. And das to work."

"He even taught me how throw knife. And play craps. And mix cement."

"You undahstand what I'm saying to you, boy?" Dad cleaned his teeth with a toothpick and made a loud sucking sound through his teeth. "Whooo, your mothah's abalone. So 'ono. Can't get enough of dat ting." He leaned over slightly to the right side of the chair and laid a gigantic fart. "How much money you need?"

"Two hundred dollars."

"Money is hard to come by. Gotta work hard. People like me,

we work hard for what we get. Uncle Martin, he thought he could go da easy way, take shortcuts. Den, when he started losing and people got aftah his tail, he run away. Only one way for make money. For people like us, no such ting as shortcut. No forget dat. Das important."

"Kay."

"Dat Artemus Gordon. Da buggah crack me up." Dad reached for his wallet on the coffee table and took out a crisp twenty. He handed me the bill and I could smell the new money smell, almost like house paint.

"Thanks," I said. "Where you got dis?"

Dad dropped the toothpick into the opening of the empty beer can.

"Poker game."

———

A FAT, DARK man in blue jeans and no shirt was tearing up the asphalt in the middle of School Street with a loud pneumatic drill. The man wore a yellow hard hat, an orange vest, gloves, and earmuffs. Next to him was a big cop, his arms folded. In front of the men was an open manhole with a yellow ladder leading down under the street. Five or six traffic cones were placed around the opening. I tried to look down into the hole, hoping to see the pipes and the sewers and the large rats and alligators Uncle Martin used to say lived under the roads. Alligators big as fire engines.

"What you doing?" I asked the guy with the drill when he took his earmuffs off.

Both men looked at me. The guy with the drill said, "Gotta put in some new pipes undah here." He bent down close to my ear and shouted because he was still hearing the drill even though he had turned it off.

"No need shout, brah," I said. "I ain't deaf."

"If dis street flood, big trouble."

"Need help?"

A black Volkswagen with a chopped roof and no covering over the silver engine raced down the street. A Vega followed, with surf racks and two twin-fin boards.

"Wha? Help?" His breath smelled like cigarettes and black coffee.

"I can drill and help fix da pipes."

"Sorry, brah," said the man. "Come back in ten, fifteen years."

"By den Uncle Martin going be out of da hospital . . ."

"Uncle who?"

"Uncle Martin. He used to wrestle sharks. He'd poke out da eyes with his fingers." The cop started to laugh. "What you laughing at?" I said.

The cop said something, but the fat man turned on the drill and the street started shaking again and I couldn't hear what he was saying, so I left. I sat on the sidewalk a long time and watched the cars pass. I didn't see what the hell was so funny about Uncle Martin fighting sharks, plucking the eyes out and everything.

I DIDN'T SEE Cheryl for a while because I didn't want to give her the impression that I was some sort of creep following her around and breathing down her neck, but a week and a half is a pretty long time to be away from the woman you love, so I decided to go over to the Fitsimmons' house. The two brats were splashing around in an inflatable pool near the driveway. There were pictures of yellow ducks with long eyelashes and sailor hats on the side of the plastic pool. Water was flying everywhere and the grass was soft and muddy. Cheryl sat under the shade of the lychee tree, eating a Popsicle and writing something. She smiled and waved when she saw me. She had the funniest wave. She sorta held her hand up but just moved her fingers. I sat down next to her and we talked about the weather and Uncle Martin and whatever else came to mind.

"I'm trying to get a job or someting," I said.

"How much money have you made so far?" she asked.

"I don't know. You gotta ask Jeremiah. He puts all da money into dis mayonnaise jar. He won't let anyone near it."

I could smell beef stew and fried fish coming from somebody's kitchen.

"You wanna see a surprise?" she said all of a sudden.

"Yeah."

"Okay. Close your eyes." I closed my eyes. "Okay. Open them up." I opened my eyes. Cheryl held up a photograph. "Does this look familiar?" she asked with a giggle. It sure as hell did. It was Vaughn. "He gave it to me," she said. "Now I'm giving him a picture of me. See?"

It was one of those pictures you take every year in school. She wore a dark blue blouse and a long ribbon in her hair. She really had a cheerleader smile. That's what Mom called all the pretty girls she knew with nice smiles. Mom would be watching a game show on television, or a beauty contest, and she'd clap, and say, "Ooooh, dat girl. She get one nice cheerleadah smile." She said that about Cheryl, too.

"Vaughn got a D on his math exam," I said. "Me, I got a silver star on my spelling test last week."

"That boy is working too hard."

"I want to work and earn money. If Vaughn can, I can, too."

"He's a bit older than you."

"I can stack bricks faster dan Vaughn. Ask my dad."

She signed her name on the back of the picture with a silver pen and held it up. "There," she said. "How's that look?" One of the Fitsimmons brats threw his toy boat out of the pool. Of course the kid couldn't get out and pick it up himself. So Cheryl stood up and adjusted her skirt and handed him the boat.

"Can I have a pitchah, too?" I said.

Cheryl smiled and opened her purse. "Of course."

I watched the Fitsimmons brats, and one of them—the younger one—sat on his side of the pool very still. I figured he was probably taking a leak or something. Kids. They're amazing. Cheryl was still fiddling around in her purse. She took out a hairbrush, a wallet, and a small mirror. Then she looked at me and shook her head and tried to smile. "I don't think I have any left," she said. "Your brother got the last one."

"Oh," I said. "Das all right."

"Next year," she said. "I promise. How's your arm?"

The skin was still pretty much green, but the swelling had gone down.

"Better," I said.

———

TAMMY'S BARBERSHOP. That's what the sign painted on the wooden door said. Next to a Wildroot ad. The curtains on the windows were drawn, and from the outside the place looked closed. The porch light was on even though it was the middle of the afternoon. Above the doorway was a large air conditioner. I opened the door and a bell rang. A lady—she must've been in her forties—was sitting down on the barber's chair reading a fashion magazine. The lady looked at me and smiled but she didn't get out of the chair. "Hello," she said.

I smiled and looked around. There were round mirrors the size of bicycle tires hanging in neat rows along the wooden walls. The air smelled like hair spray and shampoo. There were also shelves covered with brushes and oils and plastic bottles full of colored liquids. Behind the lady was a big sink and a counter covered with scissors and razors and hand mirrors and clean towels.

"What can I do for you?" she asked. She said it real nice. She was a pretty lady, too. She wore a lot of makeup and a white blouse. "Need a haircut?"

"No, ma'am," I said.

"Need a shave?" Her eyes crinkled at the sides when she smiled.

"No," I said, smiling back. "I was wondering if maybe you needed some help? I could help you cut hair, or I could clean da razors . . ."

"How old are you?"

"Eleven."

The lady laughed quietly. "It took me eleven years just to learn how to cut a person's hair properly. It's not an easy thing to learn, after all. People always want it a certain way. But I wish I could hire you. Problem is no one comes to Tammy's place anymore."

"How come?"

"I don't just cut hair, you know. I can give permanents as good as those fancy boutiques in Waikīkī." The walls were covered with photographs torn from magazines and newspapers of men and women in different hairstyles. The newspaper clippings were yellow and brittle. "Why do you want a job, young man?"

"My Uncle Martin is sick in Los Angeles and I have to earn two hundred dollars to go see him."

"Two hundred dollars is a lot of money for a little boy. For anybody."

"Uncle Martin used to cut his own hair. Sometimes he'd cut mine, too."

"Did he really? You have nice hair. Thick. I bet all the girls are crazy about you. Do you have a girlfriend?"

"Sorta."

"Sorta? What's her name?"

"Cheryl."

Mrs. Tammy began fingering through the fashion magazine. "I used to have a lot of young men calling me," she said. "See, I used to be the best dancer in Kalihi a couple of years back." She smiled and the sides of her eyes crinkled. "Oh yeah. Waltz. Samba. Tango. Fox-trot. I could do them all. All the boys wanted to dance with me."

The little copper bell above the door rang twice, and me and Mrs. Tammy looked up. Jeremiah and Elise came into the barbershop. Jeremiah was carrying Uncle Martin's mayonnaise jar.

"What you guys doing?" I said.

"Collecting money," said Jeremiah. "I awready made tree dollars, thirty-six cents."

"Lemme see," I said, reaching for the jar. But Jeremiah yanked it away and wouldn't let me near it. It was like he thought I'd break it or something.

Mrs. Tammy got out of the chair and straightened her skirt. She walked like a lady twice her age. Then she opened a drawer and took out a ten-dollar bill. "You take this," she said, placing the money in Uncle Martin's mayonnaise jar.

"Thanks," I said.

Mrs. Tammy closed her eyes and waved her hand. "Who's this Uncle Martin, anyway?" she said.

"A con man," said Jeremiah.

"He wasn't a con man," I said.

"He was. Vaughn said so. He used to play checkers with da old buggahs in 'A'ala Park and crown his own men with chips he hid in his underwear. He used to stand around in Waikīkī and sell treasure maps to tourists. Diamond mines in Nānākuli."

"He was a custodian who made fishing poles," I said.

"Is there a batchroom around here?" asked Jeremiah.

"Wait till we get home," I said.

But Jeremiah insisted, and he began walking around slowly and clamping his legs together until he made himself look like a damn fool. "There's a bathroom in the back," said Mrs. Tammy, smiling. "An outhouse."

Me and Jeremiah went out back. There was a kind of garden, and the air was cool and damp and the wind blew through lime trees. There were picnic tables covered with potted plants, and a chain-link fence hidden by rosebushes and sunflowers. The outhouse was made of plywood and the roof was a sheet of corrugated metal. Below the roof was a wasp nest. Jeremiah turned the doorknob to the outhouse but it wouldn't open. He thought maybe someone was inside so he began pounding on the door. The wasps left their nest and disappeared into the rosebushes. Jeremiah took out a nail he had in his pocket and fiddled with the lock.

Mrs. Tammy and Elise came out of the barbershop. Elise was peeling the tinfoil off a Hershey's chocolate bar. "Is it locked again?" Mrs. Tammy asked, smiling.

I nodded. Jeremiah clamped his legs together.

Mrs. Tammy knocked on the outhouse door. "Robert? Is that you in there? Robert, do you hear me? Open this door!"

"Who's Robert?" I said. "Your husband?" Mrs. Tammy smiled.

After a while, Jeremiah got the door to click open. Inside was Damaged Bob, the guy who hung around the bowling alley. Only now he had a nasty bruise on his cheekbone and his eyes were swollen and black. His long hair was dripping wet because he had held it under the faucet. He sat slouched in a corner, his mouth open and a trail of saliva dangling from the stubble on his chin to the wooden floor next to his hands. He wore loose-fitting gray flannel pants and a white T-shirt. "Whooo," said Jeremiah, making a face. "Stink in here!"

"What happened to you, Robert?" said Mrs. Tammy. She sounded really concerned.

"You finish in here, or what?" said Jeremiah, putting the mayonnaise jar down and unzipping his fly.

Damaged Bob held the mayonnaise jar up to the light, widening his eyes and opening his mouth. He looked like a kid watching a captured butterfly.

"What?" said Jeremiah, taking the mayonnaise jar away. "Nevah saw money before?"

"What you need money for?" said Damaged Bob. The hairs in his nose were light and transparent, like the antennae of silverfish.

"My Uncle Martin stay sick in Los Angeles," I said. "He gotta see me."

"I sick," said Damaged Bob. "I no need friends."

"You no look sick," said Jeremiah, zipping up his fly.

"I sick in da head. Brain sick." He pointed to his thin chest. "I sick over here. Heart sick."

"Oh."

"So you need money?" said Damaged Bob, rubbing his bruised cheekbone absentmindedly.

"Yep. Two hundred dollars."

"Money is da devil. Da more you get, da less you believe dat. And das how da devil works."

"Yeah, yeah," said Jeremiah. "Whatevah you say."

Damaged Bob stuck his hands in his pockets and took out a ball of Kleenex that had turned brown and hard with mucus and blood. Then he took out a crumpled dollar bill with a plastic coffee stirrer speared through it. He tried to squeeze the dollar through the top of the mayonnaise jar but it wouldn't fit because of the plastic stirrer. His hands were shaking so much, Jeremiah had to hold the jar with two hands to keep it from falling.

"Much *mahalos*," said Jeremiah.

Damaged Bob patted Elise on the head and walked away. Elise shivered and wiped her head with her hand, and I thought she was just messing around but when I looked again, she was crying.

―――――――

VAUGHN HAD CUT off his long rock-and-roll hair and was now combed all neat. When I asked him why, he winked and said he was gonna poke squid tonight. I couldn't understand why he had to cut his hair all nice to go fishing. Anyway, now Vaughn sat in our driveway on a concrete block talking to Cheryl. He screwed around with the mailbox door, opening and closing it. When Cheryl turned, she saw us and she smiled and waved. Vaughn looked at Uncle Martin's mayonnaise jar. "Whooo," he said. "Eh, dat ting is getting full. Lemme see . . ."

Jeremiah pulled the jar away.

Cheryl reached into her wallet and took out the picture she had shown me earlier. Then she gave it to Vaughn, and he looked at it and smiled and ran his fingers through his hair. Then Cheryl waved to us again—then she waved special to Vaughn—and she left.

Vaughn winked at us, and Elise was smiling now. "Vaughn get girlfriend! Vaughn get girlfriend!"

"You bettah believe it," said Vaughn, staring at the picture.

"You going have baby?" asked Jeremiah.

"Planny babies."

"Stop it," I said.

"Wait till I show dis pitchah to Marlon and Mickey and Joe and Rivera. Going make dose babes dey hang around with look like witches."

"Shut up," I said.

"Who you telling shut up?" said Vaughn.

"You," I said after a while.

"Watch your mouth, kiddo."

"Make me," I said. "I tired hear you talk."

"No listen, den."

"Shut up!"

Vaughn grabbed my shirt by the collar. I spit in his face. Then he swore and pushed me and I fell to the ground. I got up and Jeremiah and Elise were real quiet. The cut I got moving the refrigerator had reopened. Jeremiah clutched Uncle Martin's mayonnaise jar tightly to his chest. Vaughn ran the back of his hand against his cheek. The spit made a shiny line, like varnish, from his chin to his ear.

"You in big trouble now," said Vaughn, looking hard at me. "Say you sorry!"

I looked at him.

"I going count to tree," he said. "You bettah say you sorry. One . . ."

The sky was clear, except over the mountains where it was gray and almost black.

"Two . . ."

Vaughn made a fist. His face was pointed toward the ground but his eyes were watching me. I thought about Cheryl and wondered who she thought was stronger. And if she had to choose, who she'd want to win. I could stack more bricks than Vaughn any day. The bastard. He got a D on his math test. Then I heard the phone ring.

"Tree."

He rushed me and landed a right on my face. My head snapped back and Vaughn's momentum carried him and he fell on top of me, swinging his arms and swearing something awful about teaching me a lesson. His arm hit Jeremiah by accident, and Jeremiah dropped the mayonnaise jar and it cracked open. Several of the dollar bills curled in the breeze like cigars and rolled across the street.

Mom came out of the house. Jeremiah was crying and Vaughn climbed off me. Mom's hair was in curlers and she wiped her hands nervously on her apron. "I just got a call from Los Angeles," she said, waving at a fly in front of her. "Your Uncle Martin passed away."

There was a long silence and Mom turned and walked back into the house. Vaughn stretched out a hand to help me to my feet, but I shook my head. Instead, I got on my knees and began placing all the broken pieces of glass into a pile. The dollar bills were flying into the yard of the Chinese man next door who stole Vaughn's Nerf football, and into the rain gutters along the street that fed the Kapālama Canal. Jeremiah, Elise, and finally Vaughn collected the coins that had fallen to the ground. The nickels and quarters were hot on the asphalt from being in the mayonnaise jar so long.

I didn't cry. I picked up the crumpled dollar that Damaged Bob had given me. The coffee stirrer was gone but the hole through the bill remained. I was having a hard time telling the copper-colored pennies from the dark patches of dirt and motor oil on the driveway.

The Sand Island Drive-In Anthem

THE BEER OR something was making my head sleepy. The three of us—four, if you counted our manager, Paul—had just put in fourteen-hour shifts at the Sand Island Drive-In and were now drinking beers and basically just kicking back under the big monkey-pod tree next to the bathroom over at 'Ālewa Heights Park. The Sand Island Drive-In is off Nimitz Highway down by the airport. You know—burgers, fries, saimin, and according to a survey taken by the Honolulu Star-Bulletin, the plate lunches with the best macaroni salad in Hawai'i. Anyway, after we had finished work at the restaurant, Rudy suggested we go over to Mr. Shima's liquor store, buy a case of beer, meet up here, and play some basketball.

Paul was telling anybody who'd listen it looked like he'd have to lay off two employees. One was the new guy—Walter something—because Walter tested positive on the Department of Health tuberculosis exam. The other person was Charlene Miranda. Paul said Charlene was lazy and had a little bit of a bad attitude.

While Paul talked about all of the people he was thinking of giving the boot to, Rudy swore about some guy in a red Porsche he almost beat up because the guy tailgated him then burned out after all the traffic lights changed. It was like there were two very different conversations going on at the same time—Paul's and Rudy's—and it was giving me a headache. Rudy was a big Hawaiian guy—six-five, two-forty—with a mustache and, depending on how late he woke up, a beard. Yeah, Paul was the manager of the Sand Island Drive-In but, really, once we punched out and were out of the restaurant, Rudy was like the leader of our group.

The other guy up at ʻĀlewa Heights that night—Regan, our cook —spun a basketball on his finger. He had one of those expensive leather balls, a Wilson that must have cost damn near forty bucks. Regan was the best basketball player at the restaurant and everyone always wanted to be on his team. He finished his eighth beer and carefully placed the can against the outside wall of the bathroom. He always lined up the empties against the wall when he drank because he said he liked the sound of the wind blowing against the cans, making them rattle against the wall. Eight beers. I was only halfway through my first one and already feeling dizzy. I was tired as hell. It took everything I had inside of me just to keep my eyes open, but damn, it felt so good to close them for a second or two. Then the sounds of everybody talking disappeared into a little room far, far away and my eyelids didn't feel so heavy. I was that tired. All I wanted to do was go home and sleep.

"I don't know what we're gonna do," said Paul to no one in particular. "We're already way too short on bodies."

"To be honest with you," said Rudy, taking a plastic straw from behind his ear and nibbling on it—he almost always had a straw behind his ear, like the way librarians have pens, "you really should hire some people fast. I mean, it's like da three of us here—four, if we count you—we holding up da whole restaurant."

"Rudy," said Paul, "how many times have I told you to stop stealing those straws? They have a word for that. It's called pilferage."

"It's called what?" said Rudy. "What you called me?"

"Better go home and get some sleep," said Paul, looking at his watch. "Tomorrow's gonna be another long day."

Paul thanked us for the beer and walked away. His car's engine was so quiet we didn't know he left until we saw his red taillights turn the corner and head down Lolena Street. Paul had one of those new Corvettes, the kind they advertise in *Sports Illustrated*. It got real quiet after Paul left. There was no noise, except for the electric razor sound of crickets.

"You awake, boy?" said Regan to me. "You're so quiet, I was worried you might be dead."

That didn't surprise me too much. See, I don't know, I was like a part of our whatchamacallit, group, but in a way, I wasn't. Like the guy at the ball game who doesn't cheer. I'm just the guy Rudy or Regan calls up. The more the merrier, you know? It really wouldn't make that much of a difference if I showed up or not. Really. I've never been real good with talking or conversation. I mean, all the guys joke around and laugh while I sit back and smile every now and then. It's like I'm watching a movie. Just watching everything going on around me. I'm not like the other guys. I can't come out with neat things to say that will make everybody laugh at the drop of a hat. I mean, I can go the whole night sometimes without saying a damn word.

Regan scratched the side of his nose. "Whew," he said, making a face. "Still get da smell of garlic and onions and raw chicken undah my fingernails. How many times I washed my hands awready? You spend too many hours cutting dose tings, you going take dat smell to da grave."

"Do like me," said Rudy. "I stick one toothpick in my bruddah's Listorine mouthwash and den I run da toothpick undah my fingernails."

"Das pretty disgusting," said Regan.

"Toothpaste work good, too," said Rudy.

"Lemme change da subject," said Regan "How da song's going?"

"Da song?" said Rudy. "You like hear da song?" He cleared his throat, raised his beer can, and began to sing.

"Pooshing meat all day long,
Trying for smile and sing my song . . ."

Rudy tapped his thigh with one of his straws, like a drummer working the high hat. Regan clapped his hands and hummed and threw in a "whooooweeee" or a "yes suh" every now and then.

"Working our ass off ten, fifteen hours a day,
Blistahs on da hand but it's da only way
To make da grade and get my pay . . ."

Then Rudy stopped.

"Well?" said Regan. "What happened?"

"Well, what?" said Rudy. "Das it. I'm stuck. I'm trying to tink of one cool ending."

Rudy was writing a song about us, about working at the restaurant. He came up with the idea one night when we saw a movie about these dudes doing some rough manual labor—laying out railroad tracks or something—and singing songs. They were really having a bad time, wearing rags in the rain and eating oatmeal with worms and maggots in it. So we figured if they could sing while they worked, hell, we could, too. Rudy was a pretty good singer. He owned all kinds of records and had just blown six paychecks on a used Ibanez guitar. Drove his folks up the wall. Music. That's where all his pay went.

"Dat song going be our anthem," said Regan. "Like da National Anthem, da one dey play before football games. We going sing Rudy's anthem everyday before we punch in."

"Da Sand Island Drive-In Anthem," said Rudy. "I like dat." I smiled and looked around the park. The lights above the basketball court had gone off a long time ago. Everything was pretty much dark except when a car drove past us on Lolena Street and then it was like we were on that old show *Hogan's Heroes,* with the spotlights shining in our faces and everybody squinting. I kept looking around. It was cold and there wasn't any moon. It seemed like I was the only one worried about the cops.

"Eh," said Rudy, all of a sudden, "what day today?"

"Thursday, pal," said Regan. "What? Forget awready?"

"You mean tomorrow is Friday?" said Rudy.

"Das da way it usually works," said Regan.

"Jeez," said Rudy, shaking his head. "Work so damn much, cannot tell one day from anothah."

"Whoo whoo," said Regan. "Friday. You know what dat means!"

"So what happens when she come in?" said Rudy, smiling and rubbing the side of his eye with his little finger.

"I don't know," said Regan. "Maybe ask her if she like go out. Movie or someting. You seen da legs on dat babe?"

She was this girl who had come to the drive-in the past three Fridays. Only on Fridays, in the afternoons. Nobody knew her name or anything but she was real good-looking and had shoulder-length hair and long legs. Sometimes she wore her hair in a ponytail but most of the time it was like straight down. Her eyes were sort of greenish and she had a long nose. We figured she was a dancer or something, because sometimes she wore a headband and she always carried a blue tote bag across her shoulder. Regan gave her the name Estella da Prize because to all of us, what do you call, male chau-

vinists, she was like the biggest marlin swimming off Kona. The ultimate prize. And Estella had gone to Regan's window two weeks in a
row. Two weeks in a row. She had to have the hots for Regan.

"You evah wondah about dis working business?" said Rudy, playing with the tab of his beer can. "I been tinking about it lately. It's
like you punch in and bang, all of a sudden, you ain't your own man.
Whatevah you tink, whatevah you feel, it don't mean nothing. You do
what da boss says, das all. He tell you cook rice, you cook rice. He
tell you clean up piss, you on your knees."

"Life is easy," said Regan. "You like money, you gotta work."

"Yeah," said Rudy, his voice very soft. "But look at us, brah. Look
what we doing. Twelve, fifteen hours a day. Sixty, seventy hours a
week. I mean, we're young. We're healthy. But look how we spending our time. Cooped up in one restaurant. We ain't going be young
forevah. We should enjoy life when we can. We should enjoy being
young. Enjoying da sun, da sea, da trees. Planny time for work when
we get oldah. When our kids ask us what we used to do when we
was young, all we going be able to say is we mopped up floors and
fried hamburgers."

"Look," said Regan. "Only get two ways for make money in dis
world. You eithah born with it and you, what you call, invest 'um
and watch da buggah grow. Or you figure out one way to make
money for da guys who awready get 'um. Das da two ways. And most
times, dat leave folks like us here cooking hamburgers."

"Dat fricking Paul," said Rudy, looking at the ground and shaking his head. "Made me clean da toilet again, today. I don't know
why. But I stay in dat bastard's doghouse. Da buggah no like me.
You know what we should do? Lock him in da broom closet. Evah
thought of doing dat? Take ovah da place. Or maybe da freezah.
Throw 'em in da freezah."

"You a crazy bastard," said Regan.

"Eh," said Rudy to me, "you still drawing, or what?"

"Yeah," I said, "when I get time. Why?"

"I get one favor for ask you. You tink you can draw me? See, my honey Marsha, her birthday coming up and I gotta give her one present."

"So you going give her one pitchah of you?" said Regan.

"Sure," said Rudy.

"You one generous buggah," said Regan. "You know what, pal? No need get me anyting for my birthday."

I draw. Just started taking it up—seriously, I mean. Actually I've been drawing since I was five. I won this art contest in high school and got a free scholarship for lessons once a week at the art academy on Beretania Street. I was pretty proud of that. I mean I had my name in the papers and all, even though they spelled it wrong. I did a sketch of a guy I saw one day at Sandy Beach. He was an old man and he just sat on the beach, watching the body surfers. First place. They gave me a ribbon and all. I never won anything in my life. Rudy and the guys said my drawing was almost as good as one of those greeting cards you see in the drugstores. They knew a lot about cars and girls and football, but they didn't know crap about art.

"Maybe we should start a, what you call, union," said Regan.

"I still tink we should just throw Paul in da meat locker," said Rudy.

"Yeah? What if da buggah freeze to death?"

A breeze blew and rattled the empty beer cans Regan had lined up against the wall.

"What time now?" said Regan. "Long day tomorrow."

"So you going do 'em?" said Rudy to me. "You going draw me?"

"Yeah," I said.

———

AT FOUR IN the morning the streets are so quiet you can hear the traffic signals change. CLIK. *Click.* Just like that. CLIK. *Click.* I stood outside of my driveway waiting for Regan to pick me up. The morning was very cold. The sky was colored a dark blue and there were no clouds over the moon. After about ten minutes I saw the headlights of Regan's Ford station wagon come up the street. I got into the car and the vinyl seats were cold. Regan looked at me and asked, "What dat?"

"Dis?" I said, holding up a brown Safeway grocery bag.

"Yeah," said Regan. "No tell me das your lunch."

"No," I said, trying to laugh. "Book."

"Book?" he said, looking at me as if I'd brought a dead cat into his car.

I'd been going over to the public library and checking out books on all the artists. I even got one of them library card deals, with my name on it and everything. Nobody could use it except me. A lot of the people I read about, the artists, they grew up like me—with not too much going for them—and that made me feel pretty good about the way things could turn out one of these days. A book a week. That's what I was trying to do. The thing that pissed the crap out of me was a lot of the color pages were ripped out of the art books at the library. Like in this one book about Michelangelo, the page with his David was torn out. I'd heard so much about this David guy but I didn't really know what he looked like. If I were five inches taller —maybe Rudy's size—I'd break the arms of the selfish bastards that did these kinds of stupid things. Anyway, this week I got a book about a guy called Velasquez. I hadn't read it yet so I didn't know if some of the color pages were missing.

"What you carrying books to work for?" asked Regan.

"Practice draw. During lunch." I said. "Art."

"Aht?" said Regan, fiddling with the cigarette lighter in the dashboard. "You no more nothing bettah to do?"

We drove through a red light near the Sand Island Access Road and some guy in an El Camino blasted his horn and said something bad to Regan, so Regan rolled down his window and picked up a baseball bat he kept in the backseat and waved it out the window.

"Aht," said Regan after a while. "Sometimes I worry about you, boy."

But I wasn't really listening. I'd just remembered that I knew a guy named Velasquez back at Kapālama Elementary School. Philip Velasquez. I wondered if he was related to the guy in the book. All I remembered about Philip was that he always came to school with holes in his pants and that he was the worst kickball player in school. When we chose up sides, he was always the last guy taken.

————

THE SAND ISLAND Drive-In was on a side street off Nimitz Highway—not on Sand Island—but it got its name because Paul's dad started it off as a lunch wagon on Sand Island many years ago. Paul didn't allow employees to park in the parking lot, so Regan had to leave his Ford on the street, next to a rustproofing place, and we walked the three blocks to the drive-in. The rubbish men hadn't come yet and the bins were full of old, maroon-colored trash bags, and soft cardboard boxes full of rainwater and tangerine cuttings from the yard next door. It was still very dark because most of the streetlamps in the parking lot didn't work. They were the kind that were supposed to go on automatically when there was no sunlight, but the timer or whatever had been broken for as long as I could remember. So they left the lights on in the restaurant all night. People driving past at three in the morning after an all-night poker game pulled in because they thought it was one of those open twenty-four-hour deals.

"Jeez, I had a hard time getting up dis morning," said Rudy, yawning, his elbow resting on the bubble gum machine.

"Today's da day, boys," said Regan, as the three of us walked to the bathroom. "I can feel it in my bones. You watch when Estella da Prize come to my window today."

We stood in front of the mirror, combing our hair and getting ready to, as Paul said, serve the public. The air in the bathroom smelled like Comet or Ajax because someone had left the broom closet open overnight. The broom closet was full of cleansers and antiseptics and insecticides, but I swear I've seen cockroaches in there big as common mangoes. I hated to look into the mirror next to people like Rudy and Regan. They all knew how good they looked, and you could see in the way they flexed their muscles and put on their Skin Bracer that they thought they were kings of the world, God's gift to women. Regan took off his shirt and started to comb his hair. His big biceps went up and down, up and down, swollen to the size of tennis balls. He whistled some song by the Cazimeros, I forget the name. Regan was one of those guys who took forever to comb his hair. He was always careful about putting on his cap. It had to be the right way, with the ears showing and some of his dark hair sticking out the front. In a little curl, sort of the way Elvis used to do it. There was a big crack running down the middle of the mirror. No one knew how it got there, but I heard some of the guys say that Rudy had kicked it one day after Paul told him to stay late and clean out the bathroom.

After Regan combed his hair, he washed his hands in the basin. The porcelain of the basin was stained with streaks of rust, and rags mottled with bluish green dots of mold lay petrified on the pipes below the sink. The plumbing made a lot of noise but very little water came out of the faucet. Regan took the tiny bar of soap lying on the dish on the basin and made a heavy lather up to his elbows, like a damn surgeon.

After I walked out of the bathroom and put away my Velasquez book, I stood around in front of the time clock, waiting to punch in. It was four-forty-eight. Each time a minute passed, the clock made a loud click. If you didn't punch in at exactly five, Paul was all over you. One day, he wrote down the names of everyone who punched in at five-oh-one and posted it on the bulletin board. That night Rudy bought a beer for everyone on the list.

Rudy grabbed his punch card and stood next to me. He smelled like soap.

"You started my drawing yet, Mistah Shakespeare?" he said.

"Maybe lunchtime," I said.

Click. Four-fifty.

Rudy had two straws behind his ear and carried an Egg Mc-Muffin. He offered me and Regan a bite, but we shook our heads. Rudy shrugged and belched and wiped his mouth with the sleeve of his shirt. Then he put what was left of the sandwich in his shirt pocket. *Click.* Four-fifty-two. Paul walked by in his tie, dress shirt, polyester pants, and shiny black shoes. He carried a clipboard and a ring full of keys. "Good morning, guys," he said, without smiling. He hardly ever smiled at work. "Rudy, today I want you to take care of the area outside. Sweep up the parking lot, that kind of thing."

"Yes, suh."

"You guys might all have to put in extra hours again today. Sorry. Leyton called in sick. And Ruth, she's got a dentist appointment. One more thing, Rudy. You're working next Monday, right? I've got you down for two to closing."

Monday was a holiday.

"But I told you long time ago I wanted Monday off," said Rudy, stifling another belch. "I gotta go visit my grandma in da hospital Monday. She sick. Da doctors say she get, uh, halitosis."

"Sorry," said Paul, looking down at his clipboard. "Too late to change anything now."

"I'll be here," said Rudy. He put the punch card between his teeth, wiped the sweat off his face with his hat, and tied the laces of his white high-top Converse All Stars.

Click. Five o'clock.

I HATED THE opening hours. It's dark and you watched the headlights of the cars driving to work and smelled the fresh pastries from the bakery across the street, and you realized a new day was beginning and the only part you'd have in it was busting ass for minimum wage. You'd think about all the things you could be doing—going to the beach, lying in the sun, maybe doing some sketching—and it's the damndest, most depressing feeling in the world. The birds aren't lined up on the telephone lines yet, and the only people on the sidewalks are bums with no place to sleep and old ladies going to church. And then, one by one, the cars start pulling into the parking lot. All kinds of people come to the drive-in, from folks in fancy suits with the morning paper in one hand and important-looking files in the other, to ladies who clean up in those big Waikīkī hotels. Just about everybody, really.

Regan threw the first batch of Portuguese sausage and pork links on the grill, and the oil splattered and made a loud, hissing noise. I hadn't eaten yet and the smell made my stomach growl. I think I told you earlier that Regan was the chief cook. You could tell by all the scars on his hands and arms from the burns he had working with the stove. He wanted to be a chef in a fancy hotel restaurant one day. He said he learned to cook when he was five, when he boiled his first egg.

Our first customer was an old Hawaiian man in a yellow, loose-fitting shirt. He had a red face and his teeth were brown with tobacco stains. His hair was short and it looked like he'd been up all night playing pool or something. He stood near the bubble gum machine with his shirttails hanging out, squinting and moving his lips as he read the menu. Then he walked up to my window. "Coffee," he said. "Black."

I poured the coffee into a Styrofoam cup and placed a plastic lid on it. The steam made my palms wet. The old man fished in his gray pants for some loose change, then he walked away. Rudy took orders from three construction workers wearing tank tops and hard hats. He yelled the orders back to Regan. "Tree breakfast specials, with extra scoop rice on each." The breakfast special was two eggs anyway you liked, Portuguese sausage, bacon, ham, hash browns, rice, and toast. The construction guys poured *shoyu* on their food and moved to a table. We got a lot of construction workers because they were always building up or tearing down some part of Nimitz Highway, around Tripler Hospital and Moanalua Park. Ever since I can remember.

The moon was still high over Waikīkī and it looked like one of those postcards you'd find over at the International Market Place or near the checkout counter at Woolworth's, next to the plastic hula dolls and the boxes of macadamia nut candies. I looked at the clock above the french-fry machine. It was a brass figure of a guy bowling that Paul's old man had won in a tournament. The trophy and the face of the clock were spattered with grease and settled dust, and the brass figure of the guy bowling was tarnished to a dull brown.

Five-oh-three.

ESTELLA DA PRIZE came in at about seven-thirty and ordered a stack of pancakes and orange juice. She had to be a dancer. That's a dancer's breakfast. We were expecting her in the late afternoon. I mean, she caught everyone off guard, with our hair messy and the sweat running down our faces. Poor Regan was downstairs in the basement stacking boxes, so I was the only guy watching the window.

I tried to watch her walk up the driveway the way I'd seen Regan and Rudy do, but I didn't have the guts to meet her eyes, so I played with the box of straws in front of my cash register, making like I was checking if it was full. I couldn't keep my hands still—I was so damn shook up—so I picked up the rag that I kept next to the bottles of ketchup, Tabasco sauce, and salt and pepper, and wiped up the counter. I hadn't washed the rag in days and it smelled real bad, a combination of mildew and tartar sauce.

She stood away from the menu and opened her gray purse and counted her change. There were some prom pictures and a Visa card in her wallet. I felt like a pervert, I mean, looking in her wallet and everything, but I couldn't help it. Then she walked up to my window. "Hi," I said, smiling. My damn upper lip was shaking. "May I help you?"

"Hotcakes, please," she said, holding a set of keys. "And orange juice."

I gave the order to Jarin—the cook taking Regan's place—and he winked and put the pancake batter on the grill. Then he flipped the pancakes with the spatula and placed them on a paper plate and handed them to me. Estella da Prize paid and said something about them smelling delicious, and then she sat down at one of the tables and began to eat. I felt funny about her sitting down at that particular table because several days before, some stray dog came along and hosed the area.

Rudy walked around the parking lot whistling his anthem and carrying a broom and dustpan. Paul called for him and Rudy turned around. Paul gave him an old, rusted chisel.

"Can you scrape up all of the gum under the tables?" asked Paul. I shouldn't say asked, because it really wasn't a question. "A customer complained about the gum under the tables and—"

"But—"

"Now."

Paul handed me Rudy's broom and dustpan and sent me outside to take Rudy's place and wipe up the tables and sweep up the cigarette butts in the parking lot. We used to wait for the wind to blow all the stuff away but it started clogging up the rain gutters. I really hated wiping up tables. We had rubbish cans all over the restaurant, but people still left their wrappers and crap on the tables. This time, though, I didn't mind too much because it gave me a chance maybe to get to know Estella da Prize a little better. I mean, if Regan wasn't around, what the hell?

The table next to Estella was covered with a bunch of half-eaten French toast breakfasts, and I figured I better clean those up before every bum within the radius of a mile was here poking around the leftovers. So I walked over and I noticed out of the corner of my eye that Estella was scribbling something on her napkin with a blue ballpoint pen. Her head was tilted to one side and her hair fell over her shoulders. In her left hand she unconsciously played with her set of keys.

"Hello," she said, smiling and looking up.

That screwed me up. I didn't expect her to talk to me first. It was like she threw off my rhythm.

"How's it going?" I asked.

"Pretty good." She said it real slow, like she really didn't mean it. She had these sad-looking eyes and she never took them off you when she talked. That made me nervous as hell for some reason. "How about yourself?"

"I'm doing okay." By now I didn't know what the hell I was saying. "Whatcha got there?"

"Oh, this?" She held up her napkin. "Just a little drawing." It was a picture of an old lady picking flowers.

"You draw a lot?" I asked. I couldn't believe it.

"Once in a while." She took a small sip of her orange juice.

"Yeah?" I said. "Me, too."

"Time to empty the trash cans!" said Paul, walking toward me and straightening his tie. The man had no sense of timing. "You seen Rudy around here? I told him to scrape the gum off the tables. Never around when there's work to do."

"I got lucky and won dis art contest," I said.

"And tell Rudy to get the plunger and check the plumbing in the john. Some jerk plugged up the urinals with toilet paper. Piss all over the place."

"Art contest," said Estella. "I think I read about that in the newspaper."

"Yeah!" I said, very excited. "Das da one! Dey misspelled it, but my name was inside. I drew a—"

"This place is really a mess," said Paul, looking at me and kicking a cigarette butt. "And get those rubbish cans emptied."

Estella da Prize got up and rearranged the folds in her skirt and wiped her fingers with the napkin she'd done the drawing on. She did it real slowly and daintily, like she didn't want to ruin the drawing. Then she gave me a meek smile and left.

So the Prize drew. I took out a plastic garbage bag from my back pocket. I figured a little later I could dig through the rubbish can and see if I could find Estella's napkin with the drawing of the old lady. And then I found something better. Way the hell better.

On the table, next to the wet circle left by her plastic orange juice cup, were Estella da Prize's house keys.

———

RUDY WAS THE tallest guy in the restaurant, so he was the one who posted the daily lunch specials on the menu that hung high on the wall. Beef broccoli, grilled snapper, chicken long rice, *laulau* plate, roast pork, turkey with stuffing, chili with frank, *loco moco*. The specialty of the house was the Sand Island Drive-In Mixed Plate. Your choice of three main dishes, two scoops of rice, kim chee, and—

of course—the best macaroni salad in Hawai'i. Four bucks. An old Korean lady made the kim chee, placed it in ten-gallon jars, and then buried the jars in the ground until it was ready to be eaten. The kim chee was just the way I liked it, with the *won bok* cabbage kinda tough to the bite and the red *tongarashi* peppers all over the place. Regan was in the kitchen making his secret sparerib sauce. He never told us what was in it. He brought the ingredients in a brown bag and never showed them to anyone. He said it was an old family recipe and his grandma would kick his ass if she ever found out he was using it at the restaurant. I was mixing the tartar sauce for the mahimahi when Paul said it was slowing down and I could go on my lunch break.

For lunch I usually had the same thing, either the chicken or the teri beef with a medium Coke, but today—you got it—I had the hotcakes and orange juice. I believe in doing stuff like that, always have. I guess you can call me superstitious.

I walked into the crew room with the hotcakes and orange juice. The place always had the slightly rancid smell of sour milk that had spilt on the floor a long, long time ago. The room was full of plastic crates that the cartons of orange juice and sandwich buns and eggs came in. We used those crates for tables and footstools. The floor was covered with old comic books and box scores from the past three weeks and movie ads with the times circled in red ballpoint pen and dust balls the size of big marbles. Rudy used to hang up *Penthouse* and *Club* magazine centerfolds he bought secondhand at the swap meets, but Paul made him take them down.

Anyway, I sat on an old couch and started my drawing of Rudy. All these crazy thoughts were going through my mind with Estella da Prize's keys in my back pocket. I mean, I figured I could try and stick the keys into every door lock in Hawai'i until I found the one that fit. I thought about that for a while—a real short while—but I figured that sooner or later, she'd make things a bit easier by reaching into her purse and realizing that her keys were missing. Then she'd re-trace her steps and come back to the restaurant and I'd give her the keys and I'd be like a hero, and then maybe I'd ask her to dinner and the movies. I took out the keys. On the key chain was a pink, acrylic heart. The keys were heavy and copper, and when I shook them they tinkled and made a sound like Christmas bells.

Rudy and Regan walked into the crew room and I put the keys back in my pocket. Rudy was carrying a mop and a pail. The water in the pail was a dirty gray color.

"Damn, I tired," said Regan, his cap tucked in his back pocket. "My back stiffah den hell. Eithah dose boxes in da basement getting heavier as da days go by, or I getting oldah."

"Where you was?" Rudy said to Regan. "You missed Estella da Prize."

"What?" said Regan, his face looking as if he'd just bitten into a rotten mango.

"Yup," said Rudy, putting his arm around my shoulder. "Dis boy was doing a numbah on her. Da man is a mastah. Smooth buggah."

"What da hell you talking about?" said Regan.

I was feeling awfully uncomfortable right about then.

Rudy wiped his hands on his apron and touched my notebook. "Whassdat?" he asked.

"You," I said, happy to change the subject.

"Me?" he said. His breath smelled like spearmint gum. "Dat ain't me! Look like one of dose police sketches I see in da newspapah all da time. Da guys who rob banks. 'Last seen driving *mauka* on Keʻeaumoku Street in one late model Buick.' "

"Cannot help if you look like one criminal," said Regan.

"Shaddup, brah," said Rudy. "I ain't no criminal. I get job."

"Now," said Regan to me. "What da hell were you talking to Estella about?"

"Nothing," I said. "We just talked about stuff. Art and—"

"Aht?"

"Yeah," I said. "She draw. She one artist."

"Get out of here," said Regan. "Ahtist? Estella da Prize?"

"Yup. She just like me. One artist. She draw and—"

"So what?" said Regan. "What's da big deal? I no care what she do in her spare time. Da main ting is she get nice body, nice legs."

"She even said she would nevah go out with anybody who wasn't one artist."

"Wha? Get da hell out of here."

"Das what she said. Das what she told me."

———

THREE O'CLOCK AND the rush hour traffic around Nimitz Highway and the airport really starts getting bad. School lets out and the young girls in colorful dresses and tight jeans come over and stand around the pay phone. People are picking up their kids from school or dropping somebody at the airport and everyone is blasting their horns and yelling and swearing at each other.

"How's the chicken *katsu?*" asked Paul, walking into the kitchen.

"Planny," said Regan.

"May I help you, sir?" I said to a skinny old man walking up to my window.

"Yeah," he said. "Gimme a pork cutlet with extra gravy on da rice. To go. And one fruit punch."

"Small, medium, or large?"

"Make it a large. So hot today."

I gave the order to Regan and poured the man his fruit punch.

Paul asked if I could work an extra six hours today. I didn't have to do too much counting on my fingers to realize I'd be putting in another fourteen-, fifteen-hour day. But that wasn't anything new. A sixty-, seventy-hour work week was something I'd gotten pretty much used to.

Rudy fiddled with the dial of an old radio sitting on the counter above the hamburger grill. I don't know how long it'd been up there. All I knew was it hadn't worked in years. Someone had left the batteries in the radio and they leaked and corroded the whole thing to pieces. Now it was all ruined and hopeless, but for some reason, nobody wanted to throw it away.

I gave the skinny man his pork cutlet with extra gravy and he thanked me and walked away. The timer on the french-fry machine went off, like the buzzer in a game show when you answered a question wrong. *Bzzzzaaaarrrp.* Regan swore and turned it off. The Sand Island Drive-In may have had the best macaroni salad in Hawai'i, but let me be honest with you, we had the worst french fries in the world. They were greasy and got soggy the minute you took them away from the heat lamp. The best way to eat them was the way Rudy did. He threw a glob of ketchup and Tabasco and pepper on it, until you forgot what you were eating.

"What da hell is da big deal with all dis aht crap?" said Regan, shaking his head and chopping up cabbage, real fine, to put under the mahimahi in the plate lunches. The knife made a *tic-tic* sound on the wooden cutting board. "I can undahstand building houses or digging ditches. I mean, yeah, dat make sense. But what da hell is da sense in drawing pitchahs? If you can draw, but you no can rake leaves or fix roof, what da hell is da sense? No mattah how good you draw, if you gotta get somebody change oil for you, no sense. Why da hell spend your time pushing one pencil? People should spend their time doing stuff dey need to know, like learning how fix car, change plumbing . . ."

The dinner rush began around five and the cars started pulling in. The folks were going home from work and picking up food because they didn't feel like cooking. I got ice from the ice-making machine in the back and carried it in a bucket to the soda fountain in front. Paul was a real scientific and analytical dude and he once took this survey that said three out of four people eating at a drive-in will order a Coke. Easier to say, or something. So during the lunch and dinner rushes, when everyone was scrambling around and things got pretty crazy, one guy stayed by the soda machine filling cups with Cokes and leaving them in front of the machine so everyone else didn't have to waste time pouring the stuff. It was like mass production. Someone ordered a Coke and I turned around and, bang, it's right there, and I give the customer his Coke and he gives me his money and it's "Next, please." You see the very same thing at football games and movie theaters. I don't know if Paul was the actual inventor of this technique. What happens, though, is that the whole place becomes covered with plastic cups full of flat Cokes and melted ice cubes. The survey was right, though. We were really screwed when someone came up and ordered, say, a grape soda.

A fat lady with long black hair and glasses walked up to my window. If you looked closely at her hair you could see that some of it was curly and white, like corkscrews. She came in every day, and some of the guys, like Rudy, called her Mauna Keʻa on account of the fact that she was about six feet tall and three hundred pounds. "Uh," Mauna Keʻa said, looking at the menu, wiry hairs on her chin. "Gimme da spaghetti and meatballs, one side order lemon chicken, one cheeseburgah deluxe, fries, one chocolate shake, and one Diet Coke."

A Diet Coke. That killed me.

"Eat here or to go, ma'am?" I said.

"Uh, eat here."

I gave Regan the order and turned around to get Mauna Keʻa's Diet Coke. The problem was that if you know anything about Cokes, you know that regular Cokes and Diet Cokes are pretty much the same color—brown. So I poured Mauna Keʻa her Diet Coke but I got it mixed up with the million cups of regular Cokes on the counter. I asked Rudy which was the Diet and he gave me a cup and shrugged. "Nah mind," he said. "No can tell da difference."

So I closed my eyes and gave Mauna Keʻa her food and her

Coke—diet or regular or whatever. She checked to see if I'd gotten her order correct. Then she waddled to a table and sat down. I got the hell out of there before she came back. Paul was yelling for somebody to go downstairs into the basement to bring up a carton of napkins, and I volunteered. I didn't want to be around when Mauna Keʻa exploded all over the place, complaining that we had given her a regular Coke instead of a Diet Coke. "What you like me do?" I could hear her rumble. "Get fat?" I didn't want any part of that. So I spent some time downstairs fooling around and wasting time. It was sorta like hiding in a bomb shelter, now that I really think about it.

———

ESTELLA DA PRIZE came back to the restaurant at about seven. Now she wore white shorts and a pink top and carried her blue tote bag. I was back outside, sweeping up the lot, and I watched her with the broom in my hand as she went to Rudy's window. It just wasn't Regan's day. The poor guy was in the back cleaning up the grease trap. Estella smiled and ordered a soda. Then she sat down at a corner table—one of our best—in the shade and all, with a nice view of Red Hill, and if the weather was clear enough, Pearl Harbor.

I took some surveys of my own and I figured it took a normal person about ten to twelve minutes to finish up a medium drink, thirteen for a Coke because of the carbonation and all. I made like I was sweeping up the floor, and when Estella looked my way, I made like I'd just noticed her. "Hi," I said. It sounded pretty convincing. I mean, I didn't sound like a guy who had considered sticking Estella's keys in every door lock in town to find out where she lived.

"Hello," Estella said. "Gosh, are you still here? You've been here straight through since morning?"

"Yeah. What a way to spend a day, huh?"

"How do you find the time to draw?"

"Dat's a problem," I said, trying to look serious even though I was up on cloud nine that she remembered. "It's like all my time is spent here, you know? And by da time I get home, I so damn tired I no feel like doing nothing but sleeping."

There was a long silence. Estella nodded her head slowly as if she was looking for something to say. A large moth circled around a blinking electric light on the ceiling. "Have you ever thought about maybe drawing the drive-in?" said Estella. "Like at night or something?"

"Das not a bad idea," I said, starting to think about it.

"By the way," said Estella, looking confused and a little bit concerned. "You wouldn't have happened to find a set of keys here, would you? I asked the guy at the window but he said that someone would have turned them in by now."

This was the moment of truth, one of those brief seconds that come along every now and then that can change your life forever. I reached into my back pocket and whipped out the keys. Her eyes opened up real big and she smiled. "Are dese it?" I said.

"Yes," she said, touching my shoulder lightly. "You saved my life." I smiled. "Where'd you find them?"

"On da table. Aftah you left dis morning. I was gonna turn them in but—"

"I can be real forgetful about stuff like that." She finished her soda and gathered up her things. "Thanks a million," she said, standing up and putting her tote bag on her shoulder.

Damn, I had to do it now.

" 'Scuse me," I said, my fist pretty much clenched around the broom. "I was tinking, uh, maybe you wanna, uh, maybe g-go to da movies or someting? Maybe tonight or Saturday or someting? We could—"

"When?" said Estella. She was still smiling, sorta.

"Tonight or Saturday or next week if you're busy or . . . we could see dat comedy with, uh, what's his name . . ."

Estella put her finger on her chin and shook her head. "I'm sorry," she said. "Maybe some other time, though."

"Yeah," I said, waving. "Maybe some othah time."

She smiled, but she looked away when my eyes met hers. Then she waved and left, but I didn't watch her walk away.

———

THE LAST HOUR of the shift was something we called the home-stretch. That was usually the time everybody figured out where they wanted to go after work, whether it was pinball, or torching with a spear and flashlight, or just hanging out in someone's garage or up at ʻĀlewa Heights. Rudy was the instigator. Every night it was Rudy who'd ask what we were going to do. He always wanted to go buy a case of beer and catch a drive-in movie, or cruise through Hotel Street and see if any of his friends were getting into trouble with the cops. Even after a fifteen-hour shift. The man never got tired.

The trash cans were all full, so I went into the back to get more garbage bags. Regan was in the kitchen washing the large pots and pans that we cooked the stews and curries and pot roasts in.

"I getting dishpan hands," said Regan, holding up his fingers. The skin was white, shriveled, and peeling.

"Anybody get one screwdriver?" asked Rudy, walking into the kitchen and opening every drawer in sight. He was chewing on a straw.

"Screwdriver?" said Regan. "For what?"

"What you guys like do tonight?" said Rudy. "I was tinking we should go Waikīkī. Dancing."

"Dancing?" said Regan, making a face.

"I tell you," said Rudy. "Going be good. Friday night. All da women dat going be there. With da fancy dresses and—"

"I tired," said Regan. "I tink so I going home sleep."

"C'mon, Regan. No be one wet blanket. You sound like one old man."

"Rudy," said Paul, walking into the kitchen. "I thought I told you to stay outside and clean up the lot."

"I am, Paul," said Rudy. "I just came in here looking for one screwdriver."

"Just do what I tell you," said Paul. "And get back outside." Rudy threw the straw on the floor like a guy who'd just finished a cigarette. Paul turned to me. "And what the hell are you looking at?" he said. "Didn't I send you outside, too?"

"I-I'm getting garbage bags," I said.

"Get your ass outside," Paul said. "Jeez, why doesn't anybody listen to me?"

I got the garbage bags and walked back outside. Rudy was on one knee in front of the bubble gum machine. It was one of those red ones—fire engine red, I think they call it—that looked like it had been around for centuries. You put in a nickel and turn the metal handle and you get a jawbreaker or some bubble gum or some toy, like dice or a rubber spider. Next to Rudy was a kid, a *haole*-looking boy with red hair and an old green shirt. I figured the kid had stuck his nickel in the machine and didn't get his rubber spider by the way Rudy was messing around with the handle of the coin return. He was swearing and whacking the top of the machine with the palm of his hand. If the damned thing had been a pinball machine, old Rudy would have tilted.

"Rudy," said Paul, "what the hell are you doing?"

"Eh, Paul," said Rudy. "See, das why I was looking for da screwdriver. Dis kid lost his nickel in here—"

"Get under the tables and scrape that gum off before I—"

"Wait till I get dis kid his fricking nickel."

"Right now."

Rudy rose and banged the machine with his open palm and the glass shattered. The colorful balls of bubble gum and plastic containers full of dice and rubber spiders fell out of the machine and bounced around on the asphalt parking lot. It made a sound like rain.

"Rudy," said Paul, "you're in hot water now."

Rudy shook his head like he was amazed. "I nevah even hit da ting hard. I just tapped 'em."

"You're good for nothing, you know that? When my father finds out . . ."

"I sorry."

"I'm so tired of your crap. You can't follow directions. You don't know how to listen. You move slowly. You're stupid."

"Stupid?"

"You're fucking fired! Get off this property right now!"

"You know what I should do?" said Rudy, moving closer to Paul. "I should break your damn—"

"Get the hell off this lot! This very instant!"

Rudy took off his hat and apron and threw the clothes at Paul's feet. Then he turned around and spit between his teeth. Paul walked away and Rudy crossed the street against the red light. The *haole*-looking boy was crying. The balls of bubble gum were rolling all over the place. They looked like the balloons marching bands release during halftime at football games.

———

I WAS THE one who gave Regan the news. It was strange because as much as I knew it was bad news—terrible news—my heart was going fast and I couldn't wait to tell him, just to see his expression and what he'd do. That's how I imagine the guys on the six o'clock news get when they have something real terrible to tell us.

"What you mean, 'He canned'?" said Regan, drying the last of the pots with a towel. "Just like dat? What da hell happened?" He picked up the knife on the cutting board and sliced a carrot in half. He did it so hard one end shot across the kitchen and banged against some pans hanging in a corner. "How Rudy's song go?" said Regan, who began to sing.

> *"Pooshing dat meat all day long,*
> *Trying for smile and sing my song,*
> *Uh, deedeedumdumdah*
> *What da next line, brah?*
> *And uh . . ."*

Paul walked into the kitchen. When he saw us, he clapped his hands and said, "C'mon, gang! Let's get to work." For people like Paul, work was an eternal pep rally. He began whistling the tune Regan was singing and took out a set of keys. He then opened Rudy's cash register and counted the money. He put the bills in a leather pouch and took out the unopened rolls of nickels, dimes, and quarters you get at the bank and placed them in his pocket. Then he locked the drawer, took out the cardboard sign that read THIS WINDOW CLOSED and leaned it against the cash register. It was quiet as hell. It was like Rudy had died.

Then I got this real funny idea in my brain. I figured maybe I could talk Paul into giving Rudy his job back. Then I'd be the hero, at least for a day. It'd be almost as good as winning first place in the art contest and reading my name in the paper, even though they misspelled it.

Paul stood around, writing something on his clipboard. He chewed on his pen and shook his head. I walked up to him and he turned toward me. "Yeah?" he said, looking annoyed.

"Uh," I began. I wasn't really ready. "I was doing some tinking a-about Rudy . . ."

Regan was moving three large boxes of napkins on a hand truck.

"Yeah?" said Paul.

"Well . . . ," I said.

"What if I gave him a second chance?" said Paul.

"Yeah."

"What if I say it's none of your damned business?"

I wasn't ready for something like that. Damn, was I shaking. "Somebody like Rudy, you nevah know what he's gonna do. He's got a mean streak."

"Look," said Paul, "I have some customers standing in line at the window. Why don't you just worry about yourself and take care of the people outside? If I need advice on how to run my restaurant, I'll ask for it."

"Just give him a chance, Paul. A second chance, I mean. Can't you—"

"Take care of the customers!"

"You ain't listening to me, Paul."

And just like that, he grabbed my shirt. My paper hat fell onto the floor and landed in a puddle of water. I froze. He grabbed me right by the neck, by the collar. I didn't know what to do. And I hated myself for it. He looked at me for a while, like he wanted to whack me one, and I saw his thin mustache and the beads of sweat on his forehead. My heart was pounding and I could feel it going up and down, up and down in my throat. Then Paul let go of my shirt and ran his fingers through his short hair. "Get to work," he said. "And mind your own damn business." Then he walked away.

I saw Regan behind the hand truck, wiping his face with his hat. I wasn't sure if he'd seen what had happened. The onion and garlic smell of the restaurant was making my eyes sting.

THE SAND ISLAND Drive-In closes at ten.

Most of us usually had to stay around another hour or so to turn off the electricity and polish the fridge and lock up, while Paul sat in his office working on the adding machines and checking to see if the cash register receipts balanced out with the dough in the drawers. Closing time was usually pretty much a happy occasion, the best hour of work, with everyone thinking about going home and taking a shower and getting some dinner and maybe going out later. It was like Christmas. Tonight, though, everything was uncomfortable as hell. No one sang or danced in the halls. You didn't hear dirty jokes or lies about what so-and-so saw through the cracks in the wall of the ladies' restroom. You'd think it was five in the morning all over again.

Regan stood near the punch clock. There was a bulletin board on the wall above the clock. It was empty except for several mosquitoes someone had caught and pinned up with needles.

"You gonna do anyting tonight?" I asked. "Talk to Rudy or someting?"

"Naw," said Regan.

I got the Safeway bag with my Velasquez book and left. The night air was cool on my face. Somewhere in the mountains, somebody was setting off fireworks. When I got home, I took a shower and lay down on my bed and started reading the newspaper. It was pretty hard to do on account of the fact that I couldn't get my mind off Rudy and what he might do to Paul. Besides, my mother had cut out all these coupons from the paper, so it was full of holes. I debated about giving Rudy a call, but I figured maybe he didn't want to hear from anybody right now. We all get that way sometimes. Then I decided to call him anyway, but his mom said he hadn't come home from work yet and she didn't know where he went.

That worried the crap out of me. I looked at the clock. It was almost midnight. I tried to go to sleep but I started thinking about Estella da Prize and what she said about drawing the drive-in at night, when nobody was around and all the lights that never go off were shining. I sat up in bed and listened to the hum of the electric clock. There were a lot of nice things I could do with the shadows and wood and glass and darkness and stuff. I thought about it for a while and then I got out of bed. I asked my old man for the car keys and headed down Nimitz Highway back to the drive-in.

When I got there, the lights in the parking lot were off and except for the lights inside the drive-in, the area was damn near pitch-dark. Everything was so quiet I could hear the electricity buzzing through the wires on the telephone poles. I had never seen the restaurant like this, at this hour. But it was just like I imagined, barren and lonely as hell. The only car in the parking lot was Paul's *Sports Illustrated* Corvette. I figured he was in his office working the accounts, balancing the books and all.

I reached into the glove compartment and took out the old sketchbook I used for the art academy lessons I had won. I was actually going to draw the drive-in. I really didn't know why I was doing it. It was just something I had to do. Like when you're hungry, something tells you to eat. When you drink several beers, sooner or later you're gonna have to take a leak. It wasn't so much something I wanted to do—who the hell ever heard of wanting to sit in a car in the middle of the night drawing a restaurant?—so much as something I had to do. Drawing was just something I was born with, I guess. Like Regan. The kinds of things he could do on the basketball court, you can't teach or learn. He just had this coordination thing between his hands and his eyes. It's all instinct. Maybe that's the word, instinct. Ever since I can remember I was always screwing around with pens and Crayola crayons and coloring books and sketch pads and paint-by-numbers kits.

I don't know how long I sat in the parking lot, but I guess maybe a half hour, hour. Even though I had a flashlight, it was so dark my eyes were getting pretty sore. I could have turned on the lights in the car, but I didn't want the whole world to know I was around. It drizzled a little and the wind blew hard, but I was pretty content because the drawing was coming out real well.

All of a sudden, I heard yelling coming from the drive-in. I put my sketchbook back in the glove compartment and walked quickly toward the restaurant. I placed my ear against the heavy door and I could hear voices, but the sound was muffled, like when you put your ear to an ocean shell.

"Get the hell out of my office," I heard Paul say. "It's been a long day and I'm not in the mood for any of this."

"I like talk to you, das all."

"Get your ass off my property right now! Before I call the cops." Suddenly, there was a loud noise. A terrible banging and ringing sound. Like someone had yanked the phone out of the wall and thrown it across the room. "Get your hands off me!" said Paul.

"Shut up and listen," someone said. Rudy? Paul was silent. I knew I had to get in there before something real bad happened. Given half the chance, Rudy'd kill Paul. All I had to do was open the door, open the damn door. Why couldn't I do it? Where the hell were the cops when you needed them? "Da problem with you is dat you treat us employees like dog shit."

"What the hell are—"

"SHUT DA HELL UP!"

And then it got real quiet. The only sound I heard was the hum of the icebox generator. Damn, why couldn't I walk into the office and break the whole thing up?

"Look," Paul said, "why don't you go home and we'll talk about all of this tomorrow?"

"LATAHS WITH TOMORROW!" Someone cracked what sounded like a beer bottle and I jumped. "You making me lose my temper, Paul. I-I could kill you right now, man. I mean, don't make me feel dat way, Paul."

Where the hell were the cops? They were always around at parades or at concerts telling you to put away the dope or hiding behind some sign or big tree waiting to give you a speeding ticket. Where the hell were they now? A human life was on the line here.

A hand on my shoulder.

The cops! It had to be.

"What da hell is going on here?" the voice behind me said. I turned around. Damn, it was Rudy!

"I thought you was inside . . ." I looked at the door, confused as hell.

"I was driving around," said Rudy. "Trying to clear my head. I decided to cruise by da restaurant—one last look, you know?—and I saw your car and—"

"Paul," someone inside said. "I going take care of you now, pal. All dat crap we gotta take from you. I going shove 'em right up your damn—"

"Damn!" said Rudy, pushing the door open. I followed. The room was dimly lit, except for a lamp. Paul sat on top of his desk. His calculator was still on, humming gently in the darkness. Below the desk was a metal safe. "What da hell is going on here?" said Rudy.

"Whassup, Rudy?" said Regan, his eyes red and teary. He held a broken beer bottle by the neck and had the jagged edges pressed lightly against Paul's Adam's apple. Every time Paul swallowed, his throat brushed against the sharp glass. "I'm talking business with da boss."

"Put dat bottle down," said Rudy.

"What?" said Regan, like he couldn't understand what Rudy was saying.

"Put dat ting down before somebody get hurt, before you hurt yourself."

Regan started to laugh. "You worrying about da wrong dude getting hurt, pal."

"C'mon," said Rudy. "Give dat stupid ting to me."

"No."

"Gimme dat bottle before I kick your ass." Rudy extended his hand slowly and reached for the bottle.

"NO!"

Regan slashed at the air near Rudy's fingers with the broken bottle. Rudy shot his hand back, just in time, like someone who'd just touched a hot stove. Rudy looked hard at Regan. Regan stared back. "You undahstand what I doing here, or what?" Regan said to Rudy. "I trying for get your job back. Can't you see dat? For crying out loud, Rudy. I doing dis for you, pal."

"I know," said Rudy quietly. "I know. But—"

"FOR YOU, YOU UNDAHSTAND?"

"Yeah, yeah," said Rudy, nodding. "I undahstand. But you tink dis da right way? Hah? Den you more stupid dan I thought."

"Why you calling me stupid?"

"Put dat bottle down," said Rudy.

"What?" said Regan. "How come you Paul's buddy all of a sudden? If I give you da bottle, den what? Paul ain't going listen to what we got to say. How we going straighten da dude out? How—"

"You hurt Paul and da buggah going have you in jail before you know it. And den what? You like go jail?"

"Dis da only way we going get him for listen," said Regan. "Paul, he don't know how listen. You know dat, Rudy. You should know dat bettah dan anybody."

"I do," said Rudy. "But you gotta put da bottle away. Den, who knows, maybe he going listen. You cannot go around acting like you going cut open somebody's throat."

"I tell you, he ain't going listen!" said Regan.

Rudy extended his hand one more time toward Regan. "C'mon, my man," he said. "Hand it ovah, brah. Be smart."

Regan put his fingers over his eyes, like he was thinking about what he should do. Rudy reached closer for the bottle. Then suddenly, quick as a cat, Regan slashed out with the bottle again. This time he a made a three-inch slice from Rudy's wrist to the thumb. For a split second, maybe as long as it takes a flashbulb to go off, the cut was as thin as a red piece of thread. But then, all of a sudden, the blood poured out of Rudy's hand like it was coming out of a faucet. Regan, his eyes wide open, stared at the cut he had made. He held the bottle tightly and his mouth was shaking, but no words were coming out.

"Give me da bottle," said Rudy.

Regan shook his head. "Man, if I-I give you da bottle, we ain't going nowhere. Paul ain't going do shit for us and we going end up in da same boat we always been in. Can't you see dat? I just trying for even tings out a bit. It's da only way."

"It ain't da only way."

"Yeah?" said Regan. "How else? Hah? How else?"

"I don't know," said Rudy, shaking his head. "I don't know, pal."

"Put the bottle down," said Paul quietly. "Before you hurt—"

"SHUT UP!" said Regan, screaming loudly. I don't think there was anyone in the room who didn't jump. "SHUT DA FUCK UP! DIS IS ALL YOUR FUCKING FAULT! YOU LIKE ME CUT YOUR FUCKING THROAT NOW, YOU BASTARD? HAH? RIGHT NOW?" He moved the bottle closer to Paul's throat.

"Regan," said Rudy. "I—"

"No, Rudy!" said Regan. "YOU FUCKING WRONG, BRAH! IT'S LIKE YOU SAY, MAN! WE PEOPLE! ALL OF US! BUT WHEN YOU WORK FOR ASSHOLES LIKE DIS FUCKER, YOU LOSE A BIG PART OF YOURSELF!"

Rudy rushed at Regan and, with one hand, grabbed his neck. With his other arm, Rudy grabbed the hand Regan held the bottle with and twisted the wrist backward. Regan let out a scream like a wild animal. "LEMME GO, YOU DUMB BASTARD! WHAT DA HELL YOU TINK YOU DOING? I DOING DIS FOR YOU! FOR ALL OF US! LEMME GO!" Rudy increased the pressure on Regan's wrist. The blood from Rudy's cut hand smeared on Regan's cheek. "LEMME GO, FUCKER! LEMME GO!"

"Drop da bottle," said Rudy. Regan gritted his teeth and shook his head. "Damn it, Regan," said Rudy. "No be hard head! Drop it!"

"Don't you see what's gonna happen if I let go da bottle?" said Regan. "Rudy? Don't you see?"

Regan tried to twist out of the hold, but Rudy was too strong. All of a sudden, Regan stopped struggling. He looked at the broken bottle in his hand, spattered with Rudy's blood.

"Let it go," said Rudy.

"Damn," said Regan, not looking at anyone. He threw the bottle down and it shattered on the floor. Rudy let Regan's wrist go, and Regan rubbed it with his other hand. Rudy wrapped his cut hand in his shirt. Regan looked at Paul. "You one fucking lucky man, you know dat?"

Paul didn't answer.

"YOU KNOW DAT? HAH? TALK, YOU BASTARD! I SAID YOU ONE FUCKING LUCKY BASTARD! YOU GET EARS? HAH?"

Paul placed his hand on his neck and got off the desk. Rudy moved toward him, and Paul backed away. Then Rudy grabbed Paul's shirt, smiled, and fixed his collar. "Manager dude, you gotta stay spiffy."

"So now what?" Regan said to Paul. "You get anyting to say?"

Paul looked at each of us. It was the first time he had looked any of us in the eye for a long time. "Yeah," he said, running his hand through his hair. "I've got something to say." He started looking like his old self. Paul adjusted his shirt and tucked the tails back into his pants. "You're all fucking fired. I don't want to see any of you any-where near this restaurant ever again. Ever again, got that?"

And without another word, he turned around and disappeared down the hallway.

———

THE THREE OF us sat under the big monkeypod tree next to the bathroom over at ʻĀlewa Heights Park, kneeling over a yellowed section of last week's classified ads that Rudy had kept on the floor of his truck as a rug. Regan held the flashlight I was using earlier to draw the drive-in, and the light made a strong yellow circle on the newspaper, like when you hold up a magnifying glass against the sun. No one was saying much. Rudy had a blade of dried grass in his mouth and rubbed the skin between his eyebrows, like he had a headache. The only sound was the wind rustling the edges of the newspaper.

"Here's one," said Rudy, pointing with the flashlight. "Male exotic dancer. Perfect for you, Regan."

"Very funny, brah," said Regan, rubbing his wrist. "What about dis one? Encyclopedia salesman?"

"Encyclopedia salesman?" said Rudy. "You no can even spell 'encyclopedia.'"

"What da hell you talking about?" said Regan. "Uh, e-n-c . . ."

"Here's one," said Rudy. "Shoe store." There was a gauze bandage on his hand. On the ridges of his knuckles were carnation-colored spots of Mercurochrome.

". . . y-k, no, c . . ."

"Or dis one," said Rudy. "Guitar player. Five-piece band. Top 40."

". . . l-o-p . . ."

"You going tell your folks what happened, or what?" I asked Rudy.

"My old man going kick my ass if I tell him," said Rudy. "I can hear him now. 'My son no more job. Da buggah is nothing but one lazy bum.'"

". . . e-d-i-a. Hah!"

"Maybe we can start our own business," said Rudy. "Das what we should do. Start our own business."

"Yeah," said Regan. "We can wash car. Or open up one lunch wagon."

"We can be our own boss," said Rudy. "We no need get ragged

on all da time. Our word going mean someting. We can be like Paul. Maybe we can go into construction. My old man get all kind tools."

"Someting no seem right, man," said Regan. "Yesterday I had one job. Now I no more nothing. I going wake up tomorrow morning and I ain't going have no place to go. I should have cut dat bastard's throat. If I see dat prick on da street, boy! Bang!" He pounded his fist into the concrete floor. "I should have killed dat bastard."

"Naw," said Rudy very quietly. "Das not da right way."

"I don't know," said Regan.

"Hell," said Rudy, standing up. "It's been a long day. I gotta go take a piss." Rudy walked into the bathroom. "Baby!" we heard him say. "Ain't no lights in here!"

Regan fingered through the classified ads of the newspaper. "Ain't too much dat guys like us can do. Da only experience we get is frying hamburgers, moving boxes, sweeping up parking lots . . ."

"I was supposed to go work at five tomorrow morning," I said. "I going wake up and tink it was all one bad dream."

"How about dat Estella da Prize?" said Regan. "She looked like one machine. Nevah saw anyting like dat in my life. But I still no undahstand dat girl. I thought for sure she would be in my backseat tonight. For sure. *Guarantee.* I mean, she no like go out with me just because I ain't no ahtist?" He looked at me. "I mean, so you one ahtist. So what? So you draw pitchahs. What's da big deal? Gimme one guy who can fix my television ovah some ahtist any day."

The breeze blew and curled the edges of the newspaper.

> *"Pooshing dat meat all day looooong,*
> *Trying to smile and sing my song . . ."*

"What da hell is dat bastard doing?" asked Regan. "Dat fricking Rudy. Some guys no can take a piss quietly."

"Working our ass ten, fifteen hours a day
Blistahs on da hand, but it's da only way
I say, it's da only damn way to make my pay . . ."

"I going check dat dude out," said Regan, getting up and smoothing the wrinkles in his Levis. "Whew," he said, as he walked into the bathroom. *"Haunas!"* Then he joined Rudy in singing.

"Got da drive-in blues,
Got da drive-in blues,
Gonna get myself a pretty lady
And call it quits when I die . . ."

After a while I folded up the newspaper and followed Rudy and Regan into the bathroom. The place was dark as hell except for the glow from the streetlights coming in through the open windows. They weren't really windows, but openings on the top of the walls to let the air out. The place had a real bad smell, strong enough to make me gag.

"Eh!" said Rudy when he saw me come in. "Make yourself at home." Rudy leaned against the urinal. Regan sat on the seat of a toilet. The floor was wet and covered with soggy paper towels. Regan struck a match and it was like the darkness exploded. The bathroom began to smell like sulphur, and that was all right with me. Anything was an improvement. There were no sounds except the hiss of the burning match.

Rudy looked at Regan. "One more time, brah?" Regan smiled and nodded. Then Rudy took out a cigarette and used it like one of those symphony conductor's batons. "Regan, gimme a C."

Regan flushed the toilet.

"Good," said Rudy. He cleared his throat and then began counting off, like a drummer setting the time. "One. Two. Tree. Four."

"Pooshing dat meat all day looooong,
Trying for smile and sing dat song,
Working our asses off ten, fifteen hours a day . . ."

"Bring it up, Regan," said Rudy. He started snapping his fingers, and me and Regan followed.

"Blistahs on da hand but it's da only way,
I said I got dee blistahs on da hand
But it's da only damn way
To make da grade and collect my pay . . ."

Our voices bounced around the thick walls of the bathroom, and the acoustics were excellent, like singing in the shower or in a broom closet or someplace like that. Hell, we sounded like the Temptations or the Mākaha Sons or somebody.

"Got da drive-in blues,
Got da drive-in bah-lewwwwsss,
Gonna get myself a pretty lady
And call it quits when I die.
I said I'm gonna get myself a pretty wahine
And call it quits when I dai-yai-yai-yaiiii."

When we finished singing Rudy's Sand Island Drive-In Anthem, everybody was laughing and clapping, and the smell in the bathroom wasn't so bad. Rudy was pretty happy that the song had come out so well. It had practically written itself, he said. Regan washed his hands in the sink. Then he shut the faucet off and there was no sound except the water in the basin trickling slowly down the drain.

You better believe we never sounded better.

About the Author

CEDRIC YAMANAKA was born in Honolulu, Hawai'i. He received the Ernest Hemingway Memorial Award for creative writing while an undergraduate at the University of Hawai'i at Mānoa. He was also awarded the Helen Deutsch Fellowship for creative writing at Boston University, where he earned a master's degree in English.

His fiction has appeared in a number of publications. He is a winner of the HONOLULU magazine fiction contest, and his screenplay for *The Lemon Tree Billiards House* received a Best Hawai'i Film Award at the Hawai'i International Film Festival.

He lives in Honolulu, where he is an award-winning journalist. He is currently working on a number of writing projects, including a novel.